MW00475032

I am a [...] writing romance books was a no brainier. I live in the beautiful Pacific Northwest and enjoy it here. I am a mom of three great kids that are now adults. I am also the proud grandma of two cute kids. I started off just writing down some thoughts. They were about what my life would have been if I made a different choice. The story of Shattered started to take place. It a fiction, but I used some of my own childhood to fuel the story.

What I wanted to do was show that abuse in any form is wrong. The one that for me that is the core of this story. The story shows that words can do more damage than a broken bone. I will say this that the story seem to want to be written. I could not keep up with it sometimes.

I wanted to write about life problems and finding ways to cope with them and remain true to one's own self. That we all have a great deal of strength in us.

I want the heroines and heroes to have flaws just like the rest of us. To show that even if the world see us one way that it is not the whole story.

From Shattered came Safe Surrender, Second Chance Love, Sweet Forbidden Love, and Save our Love. I had no idea that the four other books would come out. They just wanted or more needed to be written. I place a message in each book. Some are easy to see others are not so simple.

So please join me and let me take you on a journey that takes you away and have you see what I have done. See you inside the pages.

Read what you Love.
Love what you read.

SHATTERED

Left Hand Justice Series

Anne Beck

TABLE OF CONTENTS

The world is a dangerous place.
Not because of those who do evil.
But because of
Those who look on.
And do nothing.

———

Albert Einstein

CHAPTER 1

HAD IT REALLY BEEN TEN YEARS? Driving along, she noticed that the sights and smells were the same. The smells brought back some happy memories, such as the smell of freshly turned earth ready for planting and of fresh air. However, other scents brought nightmares of horrors that no child should have to live through. The smell of mint on a warm summer night triggered a unique pain and fear in her. Of the beatings that would leave black and blue marks as well as welt marks for days. With the smell of alcohol and the screams of never being good enough by someone that should have loved her no matter what.

Why was the air so much better there than where she had been living? The smells told her she was back where she had grown up, in this state that she knew so well. It was late spring, and many of the fields were being plowed in preparation for the year's crop to be changed from wheat to corn. She could see the sheep tending their lambs as they ran around, playing.

She was now returning home to face the same things that had prompted her to run away ten years earlier. Only after dealing with the past would, she be able to heal and go back to the world she had made for herself—and go back to work.

It almost seemed like yesterday that she had driven away as fast as her car would go. Her feelings were about the same. The overwhelming need to get away from this place came rolling back. She had fled for her survival; if she had not left then, she never would have. Some said that time healed all wounds, but some wounds remained, and no matter what she did, she

1

could not fix them. These were the wounds she needed to heal somehow if she was ever going to be able to move on with her life.

The department psychologist and the Chief US Marshal had forced her to take medical leave in order to give her body and mind time to heal from her last assignment. The department's doctor had recommended she take time off, and her chief had agreed. The injuries to her body would require weeks to heal. Her body had taken five shots, two of which had hit her Kevlar vest, leaving black and blue marks and collapsing one of her lungs. The other three bullets had struck different parts of her body: one had hit just above her left breast, one had hit her thigh, and the worst one had torn through and ripped up a great deal of her side. It had taken hours to find all the pieces of the bullets. She had stopped breathing once in the ambulance and twice on the operating table. It had taken her weeks just to get back on her feet. Her body was healing, but her mind—that was something else. Her other team members on the case that night had been killed. She'd been able to kill two drug dealers, each with a shot between the eyes, before passing out. Her guilt over being the only one to survive made the department heads worried. They called it survivor's guilt and said she also suffered from PTSD.

What she was coming home to face scared her almost as much as it had when she'd left long ago to start a new life. It was funny that now she was returning to heal from the very thing that had started all of this. She was going back to the source of all the problems she had been running from all these years. She knew she needed to come home to face her demons, and there were many of them to face. She hoped it would heal her shattered heart and her soul, which had been numb and cold since the day she'd left.

She headed north up I-5 with the radio turned up and sounds of classic rock filled the car. It was late spring, but the temperatures were already in the low seventies. She was used to the high eighties typical of Phoenix, Arizona, where she'd been living. Having driven for more than eighteen hours, she needed to find somewhere to rest and put something in her stomach, not to mention the gas tank. She directed the car to an exit in Ashland to get something to eat and find a place to sleep.

There was a Denny's, which wasn't busy. She parked and reached behind her to the backseat for her coat. She needed it not to keep her warm but to cover up the gun she carried on her shoulder. To have something to do while she ate, she picked up a newspaper on her way in and then asked the hostess for a table near the back of the restaurant. Ten minutes later, she had ordered and was taking a sip of her coffee, when a commotion caught her eye. She looked up to see the waitress talking to a couple of local cops and pointing her way.

Fuck! she thought. Any type of contact with the local law was the last thing she needed to deal with. She tried to ignore them and continued to skim the paper. The sound of a man clearing his throat broke her concentration.

"Excuse me, miss, but could I have a word with you? Please keep your hands in plain sight." The officer appeared young, maybe just starting his career in law enforcement. His partner looked to be a seasoned officer, with gray hair and weathered skin.

"Yes, Officer, what can I do for you?" she replied folding her hands on top of the table.

"Could we take this outside, please?" the older officer said.

She suspected that someone might have reported seeing her gun when she got out of her car. She walked outside ahead of the two men, keeping her hands in plain sight. As they stood outside next to the patrol car, she asked, "So what can I do for you both?"

"We received a report that you have a gun. Is that correct?" the rookie said.

"Yes, Officer, I do, and with it I have ID. May I show it to you?" The cop nodded, and she slowly reached into her jacket pocket to pull out her photo identification. "My badge is on my belt by my gun, and if you would like, I can show it to you."

"Slowly," the older officer said.

Carefully, she pulled her coat back to show the badge and gun. Both officers watched and then looked back up at her.

"Sorry to bother you, but as you can understand, when someone sees a gun that is being covered up, they get scared and call us," the older officer said. "Enjoy the rest of your evening, ma'am."

"I understand, and it's no problem, but if you could please let them know that it's okay. I would appreciate it," she said.

Once everyone understood that Tessa Miller was a deputy US marshal and that there was nothing to worry about, the tension in the air relaxed.

After the officers drove away in their patrol car, she calmly returned to her table, and the waitress brought her food. When she finished eating, she paid and left to get a motel for the night.

As she sat in her room, all the memories from ten years earlier came back, including the reasons she had left and what it had taken to get to where she was now. Tessa had not told her family she was coming back to Oregon. The only contact she had shared was a few phone calls to her mom and some letters now and then. They knew she had been a deputy US marshal for more than three years and that she worked and lived in Phoenix. She loved her job, and she was damn good at it. She had begun training in jujutsu shortly after moving away and was now working on her third-degree black belt. Her mother had been proud when Tessa had graduated at the top of her class and earned her bachelor's degree in criminal justice. She had trained at the academy in Glynco, Georgia, where she had received high scores in marksmanship and been in the sniper elite class.

The closer she got to home, the more she thought that revisiting her past wasn't a good idea and wondered if it would help her get back to work any faster. After a restless night void of sleep, she continued to drive north toward the familiar homestead—and a familiar pain.

It would take all the courage she could muster to face the demons of her past. Finally, she pulled up to her parents' house, where she had grown up with her two younger brothers. She turned off the car and sat motionless with a blank stare on her face as the memories began to replay like a well-worn movie reel. Some were good, but most were not pleasant. She recalled the beatings and the belittling she'd endured as she'd watched her little brothers get away with everything. She remembered being called names and told she was only good for spreading her legs.

A gust of wind blew the low-hanging branches on the mature maple tree in front of her car, and a glint of sunlight shone through the leaves onto her face. Snapping back to the present, she opened the car door and stepped out. Judging by the number of cars in the driveway, she knew there were other visitors at the house. She could hear voices and music coming from the backyard. As she walked around the corner of the house, they came into view: her mother sitting down at the table on the deck and her father standing over the barbecue, both talking to folks Tessa recognized.

Her brothers, Jack, twenty-four, and Ryan, twenty-six, were in the yard, throwing a baseball back and forth. At that moment, all she wanted to do was turn and run away as fast as she could, but her mom spotted her a moment too soon.

"Tessa! Oh my God, Tessa!" her mom yelled as she arose, ran toward her daughter, and threw her arms around her. They hadn't seen each other for more than ten years, and she missed her daughter. Her mom was several inches shorter than Tessa and hugged her around the waist. She received hugs from both of her brother's too, but they did so a little bit too hard, and she gave out a moan. Tessa stepped back. The only one who did not hug her was her father. He just stood there glaring at her. Her mom hugged her again, and this time, she noticed Tessa gave out a groan. Tessa said it was nothing and moved away. She told them she had been hurt at work, and her wounds were still healing. She took her coat off, and that was when both of her brothers were able to see the badge.

Her mother asked if she was hungry or thirsty, and Tessa said she wanted something to drink. She missed the water here, to her, it tasted just like the high mountain spring water. She sipped her water in between answering the many questions from her mom and brothers. Some inquiries she could not answer because of the case she was working on. They wanted to know how long she was going to be there and how she had gotten hurt. Of course, her brother Jack wanted to know if she had fired her gun at someone.

What could she say? That was a sore subject and a question she was not able to answer yet. With that question, images from that night, including all the shots she had fired, filled her mind, especially the last two, which had put a bullet in each drug dealer's head. She felt the pain of losing everyone on that team and of the injuries that had resulted in weeks in the hospital. She blinked and looked around to find everyone staring at her, waiting for an answer. She did not want to worry any of them and thought it would be best to keep her response simple, so she stated that she had been hurt on duty and needed to take some vacation time, along with the medical leave, to heal. They talked into the night; Tessa only answered direct questions and did not tell them about the case she had been working on.

It was close to midnight, and she needed to find a nearby hotel to check in to. Her father had already gone to bed, and so had Jack and Ryan. It was just her and her mom now, and it hurt to leave her, but there was no way in hell she was going to stay there any longer than she had to.

"Well, I should be going," she said at last.

Her mom looked at her questioningly. "What do you mean? I thought you would stay here," her mom said, disappointed and confused.

Tessa did not want to worry them or wake them in the middle of the night with her nightmares. The memories of this place, of her father beating her almost every day only because she was the firstborn and a female, were not something she cared to live all over anytime soon.

"I know, but I will find someplace close by, and I'll be around for at least a month. I have a lot of vacation time that I need to use up," Tessa said, trying to soften the news. She said goodnight to her mom and headed out to find a hotel close by.

She headed to Market Street, just off of I-5. The hotel she found was nice and had a bar that was still open, and she decided to have a drink before bed. After taking her bags up to the room, she headed back downstairs to the bar. She had a taste for whiskey tonight, and after ordering one, she sat back in a dark spot, not wanting anyone to bother her, so she could enjoy the drink and relax a little. Tessa could feel the drink working to relax her muscles, and she hoped a hot shower and the drink would help her get some sleep. Just as she was taking the last sip, a man walked in looking as if he'd had too much to drink already tonight yet wanted more. The bartender was not able to talk the man out of demanding a drink, but he was so drunk he had trouble standing, so the bartender asked him to leave and go home to sleep it off. The man got up in the barkeep's face, grabbed him by the front of his shirt, and started yelling at him. Taking a deep breath to calm herself, Tessa stood up, walked over to sit on the barstool next to the man, and then turned to face him.

"Hi. What's your name?" she asked.

The bartender looked at her, perplexed. The drunken man let go of him and turned to face Tessa. He was having some trouble focusing on her, as he would blink and shake his head at her.

"Who the fuck are you, and what business is it to you?" he demanded, slurring his words.

"Name is Tessa. So, what's going on?"

"I just want a drink, and this asshole won't give it to me!"

"Well, that could be because you have already had plenty, and besides, I agree that you are too drunk and really do not need more," Tessa said, smiling at the guy.

"Hey, just who the hell do you think you are to tell me I am too drunk, bitch?" he slurred.

Tessa liked to be able to talk anyone down and not use force, but it seemed that was not going to happen tonight. She continued smiling at him as if she enjoyed being yelled at.

"I'm trying to be nice and let you walk away, but it looks like that is not going to work." She showed him her badge and ID.

"They don't have female marshals, bitch."

"Please place your hands on the bar, and spread your feet, sir." There were few things in life she truly hated, and one of them was being called a bitch. The bartender took a step back, grabbing the bottle on the bar away from the guy. Tessa could tell the man was going to take a swing at her, so as the guy clenched his fist and drew back his arm, she stepped aside and let him swing into the air. She then grabbed his arm and bent back his wrist. He immediately dropped to the ground, and she cuffed him. The bartender had called 911, and a few minutes later, the police walked in. After the bartender explained to the cops what had happened and after Tessa gave them her statement and showed her ID, she asked for her cuffs back. The police officers arrested the drunk and took him off to jail. The bartender thanked her before she headed upstairs for a hot shower and a soft bed, hoping to get some sleep tonight.

Even in sleep, Tessa could not get away from the sights and sounds of her last case. She relived it every night again and again. She'd watch as everyone there was killed, but in her dreams, everything happened in slow motion. She'd wake up covered in sweat, with her heart pounding out of her chest and her breathing labored. She would awaken suddenly to find herself sitting up in bed with her hands out in front of her as if she were holding a gun.

Most of the time, she was unable to get back to sleep, so she would get dressed and find someplace to go for a change of scenery—someplace with coffee and food in the early morning hours, where some people might be around. She found a 24-hour diner, where she ordered coffee and purchased a newspaper. By the time she was done reading the paper from start to finish, the sun was emerging over the horizon. The waitress asked if she wanted to order any breakfast before her shift ended since the only thing Tessa had asked for was coffee. After looking over the menu, she ordered a Denver omelet with toast. Before the waitress left, Tessa handed her a twenty-dollar bill, thanking her for keeping the coffee hot. The waitress was surprised at the amount, but she smiled and rushed to place the order for Tessa.

Tessa looked out the window at the morning sky; it was beautiful to see Mt. Hood and the Cascade Mountain Range lit up with the rising sun in shades of purple, pink, red, orange, and yellow. It was a great sight, and the air had a hint of moisture in it, unlike in Arizona, where the air was always dry.

Driving around and looking at the things that had changed and those that hadn't proved how long she had been away. Even the school was different—or was she looking at it with different eyes and different feelings? With that thought, she knew that the place hadn't changed—she had. She stopped off at her mom's work to see about having lunch later. Tessa walked in and asked for her mom, explaining who she was. A short time later, her smiling mother opened the door and invited her into her office. They made plans to meet for lunch later that day.

Tessa drove back to her hotel, thinking about what she would do next. She decided she should check back in with her chief. Tessa felt lost when she did not have anything to do. When she was at home, there was always something she could tend to or finish up; most of the time; it was work.

With all the extra time on her hands, her mind had time to wander, and that was not something she was comfortable with. It was bothersome that her mind was wandering dangerously into the past, which was one more reason to keep busy. There was too much pain in thinking about the past—from the abuse at the hands of her father to the boy she had fallen in love with. He had been her first love, and she had thought they had a solid relationship developing, but all he had been doing was using her until his ex-girlfriend took him back. She had been young and still in school, and he'd convinced Tessa to give him what his ex-had refused to give him: sex. He'd used her without a second thought, and it hurt to know how stupid she had been and how easily he had been able to talk her into it. He'd stopped seeing her, gone back to his ex, and asked her to marry him instead of asking Tessa. Therefore, she'd decided to get out of there.

She'd finished school and gotten a summer job, saving her money to purchase a car. The car would mean freedom for Tessa, so she'd needed as much money as she could get. She'd finally been able to purchase a car— the car of her dreams, a '65 Mustang. The paint was in need of repair, and the motor had needed work, but it had been all hers.

The summer job had continued into the following spring, giving her more money for her plan to escape and find some new place to start over. As her bank account had grown, she'd started to make plans regarding when to go and where. She'd thought about the Southwest; it sounded good, and she enjoyed the sun. She'd been tired of all the rain here. She'd waited until both her parents left for work and her brothers were off to school. Then she'd packed her car and left a note for her mom:

Need to find myself. Will call. Please do not worry. Love, Tessa

After placing the note on the kitchen table, where she knew her, mother would see it, she'd jumped into her car and peeled out of the driveway with excitement. The next stop had been the bank to retrieve the rest of her savings. She'd filled up the car with gas and started driving toward I-5 southbound. She'd made a budget and made sure to stick to it. She had plans, and no one was going to get in the way. She'd stayed at a motel only when she needed to shower or get better sleep, but she'd rarely stopped for long; most of the time, she'd napped in her car. She'd spent as little as possible on food and always headed south.

Blinking away the memories of long ago, she realized it was the same time of year as when she had left all those years ago. She also thought about how much she had changed, not only within herself but also in the way she felt. She took a sip of coffee and pulled out her phone; it was time to call her chief to report where she was and say that all was okay. She explained that she would be there for a few weeks, and if he needed to reach her, he should call her cell. It was time to have lunch with her mom, so she drove over and picked her up. They chose the Ram Pub for lunch. The conversation was easy and slow as they talked about family for a bit and what was going on in life there. A few times, her mom tried to ask Tessa questions about her life, but Tessa told her about only the basics, such as the house she rented and the people she worked with—just the mundane stuff and not much more.

She did not tell her mother much about her injuries, which had been so close to killing her. It had taken a few weeks for the doctors to let her out of the hospital. They'd been concerned that there was no one to help take care of her when she left the hospital, so it had taken a lot to talk them into letting her go home. Her mom was upset that no one had called her about Tessa being injured, and she said she would have been there to help. Tessa told her that she had not wanted the family to know. Besides, if she was killed, the insurance she had was in her mom's name. Tessa tried to laugh it off, hoping her mom would drop the subject. She could not tell her mom about the dreams she had repeatedly each night, in which she would look up to see two of the drug dealers with guns in their hands. It was like watching the scene replay in slow motion. She took aim and fired, first at the one closest to her and then at the one to her left. Both shots went straight into their heads before she blacked out.

Even with her physical injuries somewhat healed, the doctor would not release her to go back to work. They were concerned about the state of Tessa's mind and if she would be able to work without problems. She was told to go to a counselor to talk about it and work it out. The sessions helped with the work-related problems, but there were problems from her personal life that were a concern and would need to be worked on.

Tessa then made the decision to go back home to see if she could work them out and move forward. That was something she had not been able to do. She'd left home because she was running from her problems and not dealing with them. Her life had come full circle now, and it was time for her to move forward.

She needed to face the only thing that was keeping her from having any type of relationship and to stop trying to be the best at everything she did, from doing field work to handling any weapon she might need to use. She was able to run ten miles and complete all the physical requirements needed in training as a deputy US marshal. They had told her she was on medical leave for two months but would need to go through evaluation before being able to return to work.

These were just some of the things Tessa kept to herself and would not, or could not, talk to her mom about. The information might upset her, and that was not something Tessa wanted to do. Her mom asked if she had anyone special back home, thinking along the lines of a boyfriend. Tessa only smiled and said no, there was no one back home. With years of practice, Tessa had learned to put a mask on her face when she did not want anyone to know how empty her life was aside from her work.

It was time to take her mom back. Her mom asked if Tessa would come for dinner tonight, saying she would love to have her over and spend more time with her. Tessa hid her discomfort at the fact that it would mean she would be there with her father too, which was something that was hard for her. No matter what she did, she would never be as good as he thought she should be. Moreover, even if she told him all of her accomplishments, it would not change his mind about her; she was a female, and the only thing she would ever be any good for was fucking. "That's all any female is good for," he'd say. Tessa told her mom yes, she would be there, and she took her back to work and hugged her before she left.

CHAPTER 2

TESSA DROVE UP TO THE HOUSE, climbed out of her car, and walked up to the back; no one ever used the front door. They were going to barbecue, and the grill was out and ready to use. Her father was nearby with a beer in hand. Her brother Jack asked if she wanted one, and she said no because she was driving, but she said she would take a Coke if they had one.

They talked about what they did that day and what they would like to do next weekend. Both of her brothers asked how long she was going to be staying and if she would like to go camping with them in a few weeks. Tessa wanted to go but was not sure if that would be a good idea. She told them she would let them know, and they sat down to eat.

She knew this was the time when fights started. Her father would not eat since he was still drinking and didn't want to kill his buzz. He would not eat until he was ready to stop drinking. Knowing this, she felt as if she were seeing a bad dream unfold before her eyes. All the years unfolded in front of her as the past came rushing at her. Her mom asked him to please sit down and eat with the family. Before anyone could say a word, her father backhanded Tessa's mom, sending her backward onto the floor.

"What the hell are you doing?" Jack said as he reached down to help their mother up.

"She knows her place, and telling me what to do is not her place," Tessa's father said. Tessa could see that he was drunk and, thus, angry.

"Place your hands on the back of your head. I'm placing you under arrest for domestic battery." Her voice was low, and she had her hand on her weapon, ready for him to come at her.

"Just who do you think you are talking to, daughter, and what in the hell makes you think that you can arrest me? I am your father, and you are nothing but a stupid bitch. The only thing you are good at is spreading your legs, and I just bet that is the only thing they will let you do."

At that moment, Tessa saw red and remembered all the times he'd beaten her and screamed at her that she was stupid and nothing or no good and would never be anything. Now, for the first time in her life, she had the skills to deal with his abuse. Her father took a step forward to backhand her. Tessa sidestepped him and, with her hand, was able to block the hit he was going give her. She turned so fast that he never saw it coming; she was able to get behind him, grab his arm, and bend it upward. At the same time, she kicked his feet out from under him so that she landed on top of him. She reached behind her back to grab her handcuffs and placed them on her father's wrists, securing his arms behind his back.

She pulled her cell phone out, placed a call to 911, and then waited for them to show up. Her mother asked her not to, saying it would just make the situation worse and insisting that she was okay. Both of her brothers said the same thing.

"No, it is not okay, and I cannot stand back and watch this. Now I am an officer of the court, and it is my duty to uphold the law—and he broke the law. Every one of us has been abused by him, and I will not take it anymore," she said with steel in her voice and fire in her eyes.

"I came back to try to fix the problems in my life so that I can move on, but until I can take care of the relationship I have with him, I will never be able to move forward," she said, pointing toward her father.

"I need for him to see me as I am and not what he thinks I should be. Do you even know that I was at the top of my class in all subjects and also broke every top score they had? Do you know I can use any weapon they give me? I have a black belt in jujutsu and can take care of myself. I almost died during my last assigned case!" She heard her mom gasp.

"But only because the fucking drug dealers were using cop-killing bullets. Everyone on my team was killed except for me, and just before I blacked out, I killed the last two assholes with a bullet to the middle of their fucking foreheads. So, I would not say that I am nothing. I hear your voice in the back of my head every time I am out there, and all I keep saying is someday he will see me and will be proud of what I have been able to do. But to come back here to the same old shit? I will not stand by and let it continue. So, if you do not want to make this any harder, I would suggest that you get some help, because so help me God, if you ever lay a hand on them"—she pointed toward her mother and brothers—

"I will arrest your ass, place you in my car, drive you down to the station myself, and then move my family as far away from you as I can. You need to get your shit together, grow a pair of balls, and start being a real man, not a little boy who only knows how to use his fists and scream at his family. Do you get me, asshole?" She yelled this at her father just as the cops walked around the corner of the house.

By this time, Tessa was in a rage, and each one of her words was a small crack in the walls that surrounded her. She could feel the walls cracking, and the feeling was good. After she and the rest of the family gave their statements and her father was arrested, she turned and took a long look at her mom. She saw a woman she loved, and she was disgusted to think of all the years of abuse she had taken from that man.

"I know you are not aware of all the things that he did to me or how badly his words have affected me, but this is the reason that I came back— to see if I can work on my personal problems, which are affecting me at work. I did not tell you about the injuries because I did not want you to worry about me or the things I am going through. And yes, I left because of the things that man has said and done to me, and I ran as far and as fast as I could, hoping that if I could get away, the voices in my head would stop. But after ten years, I've learned that the only way they will ever stop is if I come to terms with my issue and work it out." She spilled everything to her mother with tears falling from her eyes and down her face. She was shocked to feel the tears on her face, for this was the first time since she'd left that she had cried. She was still shaking with rage at all the times her father had made her feel as if she were nothing.

As if a light bulb had finally turned on, she understood that she had been letting him make her feel that way, and now it was all up to her to stop letting him. She did not need to show him anything or make him see her as the best in anything. She knew who she was, and she had it in her to accomplish things all on her own, without the help of anyone. Maybe she could now start to let go of her desire to please him. As if a weight had been lifted, she began to feel a little bit freer. However, she knew there still was a long way to go.

Tessa returned to her hotel, and as she was walking toward the stairs leading to her room, she heard a man's voice.

"Excuse me, Officer. Can I talk to you?" asked a man coming from the bar area. Tessa stopped and turned to see who he was.

"Yes? Can I help you?"

"I am the manager of this hotel, and I was told that you helped one of my staff the other night here in the bar."

"Yes, but I was only doing my duty. The guy was very clearly drunk and threatening your bartender."

"I just wanted to say thanks and offer to buy you a drink, just so I can ask some questions for my report. I have the employee's report but would like to hear from you about it."

Tessa agreed and walked back to the bar to have the drink and answer the manager's questions. After finishing her drink and the questions, she headed up to her room to take a shower and get some sleep. It had already been an exhausting couple of days.

The next morning, she called her mom to see if she was okay and was told that her father had called and said he was sorry and might think about getting some help. It made Tessa happy to hear that something might change—she could always hope at least. She told her mom that she was going over to the coast for a few days and gave her cell phone number to her in case she needed to call or just wanted to talk.

The hour-long drive to the coast went smoothly, and she stopped at a few rentals on the beach, in search of one to stay in for a week. She was looking for a condominium, and she was able to find one right there on the beach, with a path leading from the back door down to the water. Plus, it was within walking distance of eateries and stores.

After taking her stuff into the condo and looking around a bit, she drove to the store to pick up some food and things she might need. She also stopped at the local liquor store and picked up some of her favorite bottles, and then she stopped for a carryout pizza and headed back to the condo. The sky was showing signs of dusk over the ocean as she pulled up. After getting everything inside and starting a fire, she sat back with a drink to enjoy the pizza.

The view was magnificent with the floor-to-ceiling windows in the great room, where she sat and watched as the last of the sun's rays slowly sank into the sea. She finished her drink and stood up to fill her glass again. She walked to the window and looked out. She wanted to be able to sleep without the nightmares and ghosts, but the pills that the doctor had given her did not work. She found the only way to stop the dreams was to drink heavily, or maybe that simply caused her to forget them. She turned, sat down in front of the fire, and let her mind drift back to when she'd first left.

Ten years earlier, Tessa lay across her bed and, with a pen and paper, started her plan A. It was not without problems, but Tessa was going to do whatever it took to make her plan work. That was number one. She was eighteen and had a high school diploma. She had her eye on being a deputy US marshal—and not just another one but the best one. She would work full-time, take courses, and sleep in between when she could—she would do whatever it took. She wanted this, and no one was going to stop her, no matter what. First, she needed to get a bachelor's degree in criminal justice and a few years on a police force. The first few years were rough, with long, tireless hours, but she finally got her degree. Next, she had to get into a training course to get her onto a police force. While studying in college, she started training in jujutsu and also did some kickboxing. She needed to be the best.

Tessa talked her way into a training facility by offering to help out around the place in exchange for jujutsu lessons. Fred, the owner, was older and helped her master her art, and she became one of the top students in the class.

He treated her as a daughter and helped her as much as he was able. He never knew about her past and always wanted to know what it was that drove her so hard. While other girls her age were dating and having fun, she worked and then worked some more. He never saw her with anyone and tried a few times to set her up with someone. It never happened, because she always said she didn't have the time.

Fred helped her get in some gun practice, as he knew someone who owned a shooting range. There were many different guns to try, and she loved learning to use them. Fred found that Tessa was becoming a very good shot. She really took to the sniper rifles and was on the way to becoming an expert.

She worked hard on writing reports and worked to make them something that could be used in a criminal trial to help break a case and put the criminals away. She worked on her skills and tried to remember all the training material she was given.

Along the way, she somehow earned the nickname Ice Queen. Many of the males in the training class were after her. She was five foot seven, had a toned body, and weighed around 130 pounds. She ran every day, and her legs had well-defined muscles from this. She would keep in shape by working out at a gym. Her hair was long and the color of auburn. Most of the time, she wore it in a braid that fell down her back. Her eyes were as blue as the deep blue of the waters off the coast of the Caribbean. Despite being young and beautiful, she held on to her plan A, and no one was going to stop her.

She never dated or went out for drinks with any of the men in the class. She would have nothing to do with them. She had a goal, and that was the only thing that mattered to her. If they found her seemingly cold, so be it. That way, they would leave her alone.

She was hired on to the Flagstaff Police Department and worked for two years while continuing to her jujutsu training. She was up to her third black belt and continued to excel with firearms.

She kept to herself but was a great team member—someone others could count on and found they enjoyed working with, as she did her job well. Eventually, she applied for the deputy US marshal program and started her training with them.

She was in top physical condition and easily was able to do all the physical parts of the training. Her martial arts black belt came in handy, as did her ability to use and master weapons.

She found that running, which was required, was a way to be free without overexerting herself, and before long, she was easily running ten miles at a time.

She maneuvered her way to the top of her class and was able to stay there with little effort. It was as if she'd been born for this. The fact that it came so easily for her made some of her peers jealous. Sometimes they tried to make it hard on her. They would never say anything to her face, but she was talked about behind her back. She didn't care so long as it did not keep her from her goal.

She moved to Glynco, Georgia, and spent seventeen and a half weeks training to be a deputy marshal, passing all categories at the top of her class. When she graduated, she asked to be assigned to Washington, DC, for the first few years, but she found that she did not like it there. When a position in Texas opened up, she transferred, and then a year later, she moved on to Phoenix, Arizona.

She worked mostly on big drug-smuggling cases. Just one year ago, she'd started the ominous case that had landed her back home and on a medical leave. She'd been working on a case against one of the biggest drug cartels, trying to shut down the main warehouse where the drugs were coming and going, when she was shot.

Her mind returned to the present, and she realized she'd drifted off to sleep. The fire had died down, and she found herself lying on the floor in front of the fireplace.

The morning sun was shining in through the front window. She had a hangover, and her head was pounding as if a bass band had taken up residence in her skull. She stood up and walked to the bathroom to take a shower.

She felt better after she had a few cups of coffee and some aspirin. She almost felt human again as she dressed for the day, choosing jeans, a T-shirt, and jacket to hide her gun holster. She would have gone for a run along the beach, but with the headache lingering, she just wanted to take a walk through the small town and smell the sea air.

She took a trip to some of the art galleries in the area, and she found some pieces she knew her mom would love and purchased them. She made her way back to the condo, and after finishing a sandwich, she took a walk on the beach. She enjoyed the smells and sights. The wind was strong that day, and the mist from the surf hit her in the face. She found a spot to sit and watch the ocean for a while.

"God, how I have missed this," she said aloud, lifting her face to the sky and enjoying the moment. A dog ran by, and a young boy called to it as he ran after it. She watched them until they both were out of sight.

She stayed there until it began to get dark, and the clouds began to roll in, hinting of rain. She stood and walked back to the condo.

After pouring a drink, she watched a storm come in as she stood by the window. She finished the leftover pizza and poured a third drink. Feeling a bit drunk and wanting to be closer to the water, she walked out to the beach again. It was dark now, and the waves were crashing in with the storm. She walked a bit farther and then sat down, feeling the mist on her face and enjoying it. After a bit, she walked back to the condo, locked the door, and climbed into bed, again hoping to avoid the nightmares.

She was feeling great and enjoying each day, but by the third day, she was in the mood for people—not to talk to but just to be around, which was unusual for her.

Dressed in form-fitting jeans, a button-down shirt, and her leather jacket to hide her gun holster, she ventured out into town. She felt the need for noise and walked to the closest bar. She hoped they had music, but not western. She walked in, ordered a rum and Coke, and found a table in the back that had a great view of the whole place. She wanted to sit, and people watch in the dark without anyone bothering her.

She watched the people as they danced, and the bartender kept the drinks coming. She had been there for about two hours, and a few guys had asked her to dance. Each time, she just shook her head to say no, and they would go away, but still, some of them watched her, trying to figure out how to get her on the floor.

A man she hadn't seen before caught her eye as he walked in the door. He was easily six foot four and had not an ounce of fat on his body. In fact, she saw only muscles upon muscles. He had on old jeans, a dark T-shirt, and a black leather jacket. His boots were like the ones bikers wore.

The locals seemed to know him and greeted him in a friendly way. He stopped and talked to several of them, and as he walked up to the bar, the bartender said something to him and nodded Tessa's way. The man turned and looked right at her. The lighting was better at the bar, and she could tell his hair was black, but she could not see what color his eyes were. He smiled, said something to the man behind the bar, and patted the bar. Before he pushed off, he grabbed a beer, and then he walked over to her table. He pulled a chair back, flipped it around to straddle it, and placed his beer on the table.

"Hi. I haven't seen you here before," he said, looking at her. It was still too dark to see what color his eyes were. She took a sip of her drink and placed the glass on the table.

"No, I'm just visiting." She felt as if this guy were undressing her right there and then, and she wasn't sure if she liked it or not. It had been a long time since a man had looked at her that way. He seemed to like what he was looking at and smiled.

"So where are you from then?" His voice sounded as if he might be from Texas or someplace in the Southwest.

She reached for her glass and took a drink before answering that she was from Arizona.

"So, are you here for business or pleasure?" he asked, raising his eyebrow and still smiling.

"Just visiting." She did not want to give any more information than that. She took a sip of her drink and noticed that he had a great smile that lit up his whole face.

"Sorry. My name is Logan McMullen. And you are?" He held his hand out as if wanting to shake hands, and all she saw was how big his hand was. She placed her hand in his and watched it disappear. His hand was warm but firm and calloused; it felt like a working man's hand.

"Tessa Miller. Nice to meet you," she said, shaking his hand. But when she tried to pull back, he did not let go; he just kept holding her hand and looking into her eyes with that smile. Her hand felt as if an electric shock had gone through it when she touched him.

He did not let go of her hand as the music turned to a slow-dance tune. She had never felt like this with any man; she felt a pull toward him. A warm feeling started from her hand and flowed through her body. She was feeling a bit hot and noticed an aching between her legs, which was something new for her.

"Would you like to dance?" he said as he pulled her up, not wanting to give her a chance to refuse.

She normally did not dance. It was something she'd never learned to do. She took a moment to think and said, "No, not really, but thank—"

Before she could finish her sentence, he pulled her away from the table and led her out to the dance floor.

He placed one hand around her, on her lower back, and pulled her hand close to his heart. She came up to his chest and felt like a child next to him. As he pulled her closer, she laid her hand around his neck, and his hand on her lower back started to move. She knew that in a few seconds, he would feel the gun in her shoulder holster. She looked up at the same time he moved over to her side where the gun was, and his eyes opened wider.

"I am thinking that might be a gun I am feeling right there," he said as his hand moved to her side as he patted her. She lowered her eyes, and a small smile formed as she looked back up and licked her top lip.

"Yes, it is."

"Okay, why the hell would a beautiful little sweet thing like you have a gun?" he asked, not once missing a step in the dance. "Again, why would you need to carry it? I mean, there really isn't much to you, and I could easily stop you from doing anything with it." He laughed as he spoke, and that was all it took. She pulled out of his arms, turned, and walked toward the door.

Just before she reached it, an arm wrapped around her arm, and before she could think about it, she turned, grabbed his arm, flipped him onto his back, and pushed her foot firmly against his neck.

"This beautiful little sweet thing just took your punk-ass down. Now stuff that in your pipe and smoke it, asshole!" She turned and walked out the door, not once looking back.

*   *   *

The entire bar erupted with laughter as Logan just lay there, wondering what the hell had just happened.

"Hey, Logan, did that little bit of a female turn the tables on you?" The man behind the bar chuckled.

Logan turned to stand up and adjust his jacket, and then he placed his hands on his hips and looked at the door, shaking his head. A small smile turned up the corners of his mouth. Wow what a woman, was all he was thinking. He walked to the door, pushed it open, and stepped out into the night. He first looked up the street and then down until he spotted her. He started walking toward the woman who was moving away from him swiftly.

CHAPTER 3

THE COLD AIR HELPED TO SOBER Tessa up a bit, and so did the anger coursing throughout her body. "How in the hell could I let that happen to me? If I ever see him again, I swear," she said to herself. Suddenly, she heard someone walking toward her—it sounded more like a herd of elephants quickly stomping nearer. As the person was just about on her heels, she turned with her gun in hand, pointing it at whoever was following her.

"Stop!"

Logan stopped with his hands up. "Hey, I really did not mean anything back there, I was just joking with you."

She placed the gun back in the holster and turned to continue to walk back to the condo. She heard him continue to walk after her, and soon he was right next to her.

"So why do you carry a gun, and how in the hell did you learn to make those moves?"

Tessa continued to walk without answering him at first, hoping he would take a hint and stop following her. After a few minutes, when he did not leave, she spoke.

"Go away and leave me alone," she told him When he just continued to walk beside her and kept asking her the same questions as to why she had a gun and how she was able to do that to him.

"I have been training in martial arts for about ten years, and I am a deputy US marshal. Now will you go away and just leave me alone?" she said without stopping.

Logan stopped, stood with his hands on his hips, and gave a slow whistle before saying, "No shit. Really?"

Tessa stopped, turned around with her hands on her hips, and rolled her eyes. "Yes, now go away. I need to go home and get some sleep."

Then, looking at her side and placing her hand over it, she said, "Damn!" She was below a streetlight, and Logan could see what he thought might be blood on her hand. Logan's first thought was to help her, and the next was to wonder why she was bleeding.Logan quickly stepped up to her and took her hand to get a look at it.

"Hey, is that blood? Do you need to go to the hospital? I can drive you; my truck is right over there." He pointed to a truck and took a step closer. He grabbed her elbow, trying to get her to move over to his truck, but she pulled away and continued in the same direction she had been walking.

"Hey! Let me help you. I can drive you to the ER—it's no problem. I know how to get to the hospital. I live in this town," he said, walking with her and trying to get her to stop so that he could take a look and see how bad her injury was.

"No, it's fine. I can take care of it back at the condo. Thanks anyway. Now just go away," she said over her shoulder as she continued to walk.

Logan stood there with his hands on his hips, wondering what the hell was going on and shaking his head. He took a deep breath and jogged up to her, trying to keep up with her pace.

"No, you need medical help, and I would be happy to drive you. Come on—what do you say?"

Tessa stopped, which gave Logan a start. She raked one hand through her long hair and then twisted around, facing Logan. The buzz from the drinks was long gone, and all she wanted now was sleep.

"Thanks, but no thanks. I can take care of it. Really, it is not that bad. Now please go away."

"No. If you will not let me take you to the hospital, at least let me make sure you get home okay. I mean, I do not want to read in the paper tomorrow that they found some woman who bled out on the streets."

"Fine, but as soon as I am home, you will leave, right?" Tessa was pissed that this guy would not leave her alone.

Logan only smiled, and they walked on, with Logan keeping an eye on her to make sure she was okay. He was ready to lift her up and take her to his truck if she should pass out. As they reached the condo, she looked down to see that the wound had almost stopped bleeding. She did not want him to know where she was staying, but if this was the only way to get rid of him, she saw it as the lesser of the two evils. She thought that she must have pulled it apart when she twisted and flipped this man over her shoulder.

"Okay, I am safe, so now you can go." She turned to unlock the door. She opened it, stepped inside, and blocked the entry with her body. She thanked him as she shut the door and locked it. Logan just stood there and stared at the door, not knowing why he felt the need to protect her or why he wanted to break the door down just to make sure she really was okay. He took a deep breath, turned around, and walked back to his truck to drive home.

Tessa moved to the bathroom to check the wound and clean it up. The bleeding had stopped, so she cleaned it and placed a new bandage on it. She changed into her sleepwear, which was a large T-shirt, and then climbed into bed, hoping for sleep. It came quickly, due to all the fresh air and relaxation earlier, she supposed.

CHAPTER 4

LOGAN COULD NOT GET HER OUT of his head all night—the long auburn hair, the slim waist, the nice tits. She came up to the top of his chest, and her ability to flip him onto his back in the middle of his bar astonished him. Her eyes were the color of a deep blue ocean, and each time he looked into them, he felt as if he was falling in. Her body fit his perfectly, and he loved her curves. Her tits were great—the right size for his hands—and he saw strength and an iron will in this woman that intrigued him.

He had just about picked her up against her will and driven her to the hospital, but he'd thought better of it; after all, she had a gun. But he'd come close to kissing her just to see if those plump lips were as soft and sweet as they looked. He knew he was not going to get any sleep because he couldn't stop thinking about her. It was in his nature to protect and care for women in his life.

That was something his mom and two sisters had made sure of after the death of his father. It was just five years ago that his father had died, and he'd had to take over the family business.

He drove back to his home, which sat high on a bluff overlooking the Pacific Ocean, and knowing he would not get any sleep, he made some coffee and worked on the mountain of paperwork piled on his desk. He sat working and waiting for the sun to come up so that he could drive back to her condo to see if she was okay.

* * *

Tessa woke covered in sweat, her heart pounding with the same nightmares she had had for several weeks now. She knew that sleep would not come now, and with only a few hours until sunrise, she made coffee, wishing she could go for a run. However, with the injury reopened, she did not think running was a good idea. She was wound up, and in need of something physical to help with the feeling, but with no exercise equipment there, she had to wait. When the first ray of light started to show, she could not take it any longer. She decided to step out to take a walk on the beach, knowing that walking would not hurt the injury, and maybe the ocean and the wind would help with all the stress she was feeling.

Logan had driven over to her condo, and he sat in his truck in the parking lot. He saw the lights on, so he thought she was up. He picked up a box of doughnuts and a thermos of coffee, climbed out of his truck, walked up to the front door, and knocked. Tessa was just putting her jacket on and picking up her keys to go on her walk on the beach when she heard the knock. She thought it strange, as no one knew she was there. She opened the door and saw a large man wearing jeans, a black T-shirt, a leather jacket, and boots. He was wearing sunglasses, so she was unable to see what color his eyes were.

The only thought that came to her was *Tall, dark, and dangerous.* His hair curled just below his ears, and as he took off the sunglasses, she found herself staring into a pair of bright green eyes.

He noticed that she had her jacket on but no shoes. Was she getting back or just leaving? And how was she doing? She looked as if she had not slept well last night.

"What do you want?" she asked after taking a deep breath. She said it with more rage than she'd intended, but she was tired, and without sleep, she was a bear.

"I wanted to make sure that you were all right, and I have doughnuts and coffee as a peace offering," he said with a smile.

"Hmm, right," she said, holding up her full coffee cup.

"Well, at least I have the doughnuts," he said, stepping forward and moving past her into the entryway.

"Hey! Just what the hell do you think you are doing? I did not ask you in."

"Yeah, but you were going to, right?" he replied, giving her a shy smile.

She closed her eyes, took a deep breath, and then opened them. After closing the front door, she turned to see Logan eyeing the cups.

"Can I help you?" she said, leaning against the door.

"Thanks. Hey, nice place here. Do you own it?" he asked, taking his jacket off and placing it over a chair. Again, she was able to see his T-shirt show off all the muscles he had. Logan helped himself to a cup, pouring some coffee from the thermos.

"No, I am just renting, and it is up today at eleven o'clock, so I will be leaving then."

He'd thought he might have more time to see why he felt this pull toward her. Hearing that she might be leaving and that he would not be seeing her was upsetting.

"So, does that mean you are leaving town today?" he asked. "I was hoping to take you to lunch or dinner to get to know you better and to say sorry about last night. I was being an ass."

He hoped she would agree and found himself holding his breath, waiting for her to answer.

"I need to be going. I still need to shower and pack soon," she said, not wanting him to know that she was really going for a walk and had plenty of time to shower and pack.

"How about you do that, and then I can take you out for breakfast? I know a great place that serves the best food, and it is only twenty minutes from here. So, what do you say?" he said.

She thought that food did sound good and that she could be done in about thirty minutes.

"Okay, I'll be about thirty minutes, so do you want to meet someplace?"

"Actually, I was going to wait here. Go ahead and take your shower and pack. I am in no rush," he said, smiling. He sat down on the couch to get comfortable.

She slightly glared at him for a moment before grabbing her gun, walking to the bedroom, shutting the door, and locking it. She quickly showered, dressed, and packed her suitcase. True to her word, thirty minutes later, she was ready to go. He was impressed; any other woman would have taken hours to do all that.

She looked breathtaking in a button-up shirt tucked into jeans that molded her hips and ass and showed off her long legs. She had slipped on her black cowboy boots, and as she was putting on her holster before the leather jacket, he saw the badge on her belt.

She started to pick up the suitcase, but Logan reached over and picked it up before she could reach it. She had cleaned the kitchen and taken out the garbage earlier. She walked out and made sure the door was locked. She then walked over to her midnight-blue '65 Mustang to open the trunk so that Logan could place her bag in it.

"Nice car; I like the color," he said as he closed the trunk.

"Thanks. I had it restored back to what it looked like right off the lot. The color helps with stakeouts. Plus, it has a racing engine in it," she said proudly.

Logan walked around to look inside and noticed a police scanner and some other equipment he didn't recognize.

"Okay, where are we going?" she asked. "I'll follow you."

"My house is not far from here; you can drop off your car there, so we can talk on the way," he said.

Not sure if that was a great idea, she just nodded to agree that she would follow behind Logan. They drove up a road that twisted and turned for a couple miles before it ended at the top of a bluff overlooking the ocean.

The house was breathtaking and had a spectacular view overlooking the ocean. Tessa parked in front of a four-car garage and stepped out of the Mustang. She hesitantly walked over to the passenger side of Logan's truck, where he greeted her by opening the door for her. She made a mental note of his chivalrous gestures, wondering how long he could keep them up.

After she climbed in, he shut the door, and she had her seat belt on by the time he got in. Logan started the engine and backed out of the driveway to go back the way they had come. Tessa noticed that there were no other houses on this road.

"So, is your house the only one on this road?" she inquired.

"Yes, I like the isolation and privacy," Logan replied. Tessa found it interesting that he was in need of privacy. She was thinking of a way to ask what type of business he owns without looking too nosy.

Logan drove down to the highway, and about twenty minutes later, he turned into a parking lot beside a small rustic restaurant. Logan hurried to open Tessa's door, and a delicious aroma wafted through the air the moment the door was opened. He led her to the restaurant entrance and followed her in. Seconds later, she heard someone call his name. An older man stepped out from behind the main counter and reached out to shake Logan's hand.

"Hey, Bill!" Logan said, and he turned to introduce them. "Tessa, this is Bill. He owns the place. Bill, this is my new friend Tessa."

Bill gestured for the pair to seat themselves at a table near a window that overlooked the bay. The waitress greeted Logan by name and took notice of Tessa as she took off her jacket. The holster and badge were in plain view for anyone to see now.

As Tessa settled into her seat, the top buttons on her shirt popped open, giving Logan a clear view of her lacy black bra. One of the few things Tessa enjoyed about being a woman was secretly wearing sexy bras and panties beneath practical outer garments. Logan gave her a wink and a grin when she looked up from her menu. Confused, she followed his eyes down to her blouse.

"What, are you still in high school? Really!" she said, not one bit impressed with his immaturity. Logan tried to stifle a chuckle as she reached down to button her shirt.

Two local officers walked in. They both knew Logan and walked over to say hello. At about the same time, both noticed Tessa's holstered gun, and they instinctively slowed their pace as they approached the table. Logan looked up as they neared, and he stood to shake their hands and then turned to introduce them to Tessa. The expressions on their faces turned from concern to relaxed as Logan informed them that Tessa was a deputy US marshal.

He invited the officers to join them for breakfast. Tessa was relieved to partake in the small talk that shifted Logan's attention away from her for the time being. An hour later, both officers said they had to get back to work, said goodbye, and left. Logan paid their portion of the tab, and they walked back to his truck. As they were driving back to his house, Logan tried to think of some way to keep her in town for a few more days.

When Logan drove to park in front of the garage, he asked, "Hey, would you like to see the inside of the house? The view is phenomenal."

Tessa turned and looked at him and then turned back to look at the house. "I suppose that would be okay."

As Logan unlocked the front door and disarmed the security system, Tessa looked around to see a staircase leading to a second story as well as down to a lower floor. As she stepped in toward the main living area, her attention was drawn to a panel of ceiling-to-floor windows that spanned the western wall, with a sliding glass door leading out to a deck. The deep blue-green waters of the Pacific filled her view as she stepped out onto the wooden deck. Ten-foot-high storm-glass panels surrounded her, but still, the wind made its way in to whip her hair into her face. She spotted the makings of a storm rolling in—and fast.

Logan walked out and stood behind her, when he noticed the dark clouds and white-capped waves blowing toward shore.

"It is breathtaking, but I see nasty weather coming. It looks to be moving in quickly, so I should be going before I get caught up in it," she said. She turned and almost walked into Logan not knowing he was standing right behind her. Logan had to grab her arms to keep her from falling back.

The only thing Logan thought was breathtaking was the woman standing in front of him. She smelled like the refreshing sea air during the calm after a storm. He was trying to think of some way to keep her there. He wasn't ready yet for her to leave.

"What about staying here until it blows over? At the rate the storm is moving, you'll be caught in it long before you make it over the mountain pass. Listen, I could throw a couple steaks on the grill later and light a fire in the fireplace, and we can enjoy nature's show. I've even got a guest bedroom," he said. "I really am an okay guy; even the local cops will tell you I'm safe. So, what do you say?" he added, hoping she'd let her guard down enough to stay.

She turned back to assess the situation and admitted to herself that she would love to watch the storm from there. She had always loved the ocean and admired its beauty. There was something riveting about all the power and strength that churned up the waters in this type of weather. She had to agree that she would not be able to outdrive it. But to stay there—was she really considering it? She looked over her shoulder at him as he innocently raised his hands.

"Honest—I will be nothing but a gentleman," he said, flashing his most convincing smile.

"Okay, it would be the wise thing to do—but remember, I can still take you down!" she replied, trying to sound reluctant and giving him her best hard-ass expression.

He took her on a quick tour of the rest of the house. On the main floor were the great room, kitchen, and dining room and his home office. One floor up were four bedrooms, two with expansive ocean views. The room next to the master was spacious and elegantly furnished. A dark blue quilt covered the bed. Matching drapery lined a large window next to it.

A door led to a private bathroom adorned with blue and turquoise tiles, a claw-foot bathtub, and a separate shower. Logan told Tessa she could have this room if she liked, and then he led her down to the end of the hall. He'd saved the master bedroom for last, which boasted dark cherrywood furniture with red-and-black upholstery and window dressings. The master bath was inviting, with an oversized Jacuzzi tub set next to a window with a view of the ocean. Tessa admired his sense of style as she observed the Italian tile work that complemented the colors in the bedroom.

They then returned downstairs, making their way to the bottom floor. There he showed off a small indoor pool, spa, and weight room, as well as a lounge area with a wet bar, pool table, and comfortable seating around a large flat-screen television.

"Very nice. I might need to try my hand at a game of pool later."

"After I beat you at that pool game, you might enjoy the swimming pool. The salt water is very good for the skin," Logan teased. "Most of the time, I only wear my birthday suit, but again, it is usually just me here." He laughed.

"Nice try there, slick, but I still have an open wound, and salt water is not the best treatment for that. And I am not into swimming nude anyway."

"Hey, I didn't mean that we would be in there together. You can have it all to yourself. But you are right about the open wound. How is it doing by the way? Need me to look at it?" Logan asked.

"It is fine, and no, you do not need to look at it. Thanks anyway," she said as she turned to leave the lounge. As they walked back upstairs, he asked if she would like anything to drink. It was a bit early for anything stiff, so she asked for a soda.

As they sat watching the storm move in, she was glad she had decided to stay where it was warm and dry. Later, they played several rounds of pool. Tessa had not played for a long time, and Logan was able to beat her at eight out of ten games.

By then, they'd worked up a bit of an appetite. Logan started the grill for the steaks as Tessa put together a salad and a couple baked potatoes. The meal was simple, just the way she liked it. She found herself relaxing more and more as the evening passed.

"You really have a great view up here. Plus, you don't need to worry about the waves crashing into the house."

Logan couldn't help but stare at her as she looked out at the storm. He could not put his finger on it, but there was something inside tugging at him to protect and care for her. The word *mine* kept running through his mind. He knew she was capable of protecting herself physically, but he detected a soft vulnerability beneath her hard outer shell, and that was where she was hurting the most. He supposed that she had built a wall around her to keep others out and that she must have been hurt to the point where she needed the wall to show others, she was strong. There were times when he could see a great sadness in her eyes, but just as quickly, the mask returned to her face.

He wanted to get to know her better, to know all about her inside and out. He yearned to take the sadness from her eyes and to make her laugh and smile.

As Tessa watched the storm rage outside, she couldn't help but feel as if a storm were constantly brewing inside of her as well. The waves swelled and crashed to the shore just like the push and pull of her emotions, and the black clouds blocked the sun much like the internal shadow that continually prevented her from feeling happiness. She was discouraged by the darkness of her memories, which made it difficult for her to connect with anyone or ever feel true joy.

She raised her head to see Logan's intense but gentle stare. *What is it that he sees in me, and why do I feel the need to be around him? How can he make me feel so safe, as if I can trust that he won't hurt me?* she wondered. She was trying to fight off old feelings that she had buried long ago, memories she knew should be kept buried. If she let them free, their release would only lead her to a dangerous place she was convinced she wouldn't be able to flee from.

"How about I start to clean up?" she suggested.

Logan was so captivated with looking at her that at first, he wasn't sure what she had said. He understood when she started to pick up the plates and wine glasses.

"No, that's okay. I can clean up later. You're my guest."

"I think it is only fair—I mean, to help to pay you back for letting me stay."

"That's not necessary, but I suspect you aren't going to give in. Okay, but I will help, so it won't take as long," he said, smiling back at her.

As they cleaned up the kitchen, making small talk, Logan stole opportunities to brush up against her. Tessa tried to place a bowl up on the top shelf, but it was just beyond her reach. Logan reached over to do it for her, and his hip brushed up against hers. Startled, she looked up at him and raised an eyebrow at him. Logan turned and was chest to chest with her, and an overwhelming need to pull her into his arms and taste her lips came over him. Tessa watched his eyes turn to a stormy green and felt a sudden desire wash over her. She had a sense that he was going to kiss her. She snapped back to reality, breaking the spell; she needed to protect her heart as she took a step back.

She moved into the great room and stood looking outside, but night had fallen, and there wasn't much to see. Still, she felt safer there than she had when she had been close to his body. She could see him in the reflection of the glass, walking up behind her. Just as he started to place his hands on her shoulders, Tessa stepped to the side to pick up her wine glass and take it to the kitchen for a refill.

The phone rang, breaking the silence, and Logan went to answer it. This gave her the time she needed to shore up those walls that Logan had threatened to crack. She needed to be strong. She was afraid that no good would come from letting him in. She decided to redirect the mood by asking about his work. After Logan finished the phone call, she asked him, "What exactly is it that you do for a living?"

"I own several businesses. I run a land-development company covering most of the Pacific Northwest. When my father died, I stepped up to fill his shoes, and it's kept me pretty busy. I found time to start a personal security business, which is more of my passion. Between the two, I end up traveling around the country, so owning a private plane and a couple other houses has made it more manageable. But I enjoy the coast and this house, so ultimately, this is where I spend most of my time."

"So, I take it you have a few bucks to your name then," she teased after taking a sip of wine, looking at him over the rim of her glass.

"Yeah, enough to keep me from being homeless, I guess," Logan said with a chuckle.

The conversation moved on to the different types of developments he'd procured and the places he had traveled to. Soon the hours seemed to have flown by, and Tessa's watch told her that it had gotten late. She also noticed that her body was telling her it was time for some sleep.

"Well, I think I will turn in for the night. Thank you again for dinner and your hospitality." She stood up and turned toward the stairs.

"You know, the view from my room is the best, and the bed is a king, so there's plenty of room." His smile was as sexy as sin.

"Oh, it would take more than a great view and a big bed to lure me in, slick. But nice try, and good night," she said as she climbed the stairs.

Logan turned off the lights and stood to look out the window as he finished his drink. He suddenly felt alone now that she was no longer in the same room with him. He usually enjoyed his time alone, and another thought came to him: he had never had a woman here other than his sisters and mother. How had it ended up that she was the first, and why under these circumstances?

He took their glasses to the kitchen and figured it was late enough that he should also try to get some sleep. He made his way to the master bedroom, stripped down to his boxers, and climbed into bed. Knowing she was right next door but inaccessible was killing him.

Tessa took a hot shower in the hopes that it would help her sleep. She was concerned that he might hear her scream from the nightmares. As they both drifted off to sleep, the storm continued to build, culminating with thunder, lightning, wind, and rain.

CHAPTER 5

THE THUNDER CRACKED, AND TESSA'S NIGHTMARE slowly crept in. It began as usual, but then, as the gunfire exploded around her, the ground shook, and the light flashed like the shots from the guns all around her. This time, the dream seemed different; it had never happened quite like this before. Frozen, she watched as her teammates were executed one by one. The gunshots rang louder than ever before, and the blood glistened with a red so deep she was mesmerized by it. The blood seeped from the bodies into puddles on the floor. She looked down at her hands, and they were covered in blood, but she was paralyzed; she couldn't run to escape. She awoke with a sudden jerk and let out a shrill scream before she could even open her eyes.

A loud crack of thunder woke Logan, followed by a bright flash of lightning a second later. Another wave of thunder shook the walls of the house. In the wake of the sounds of the storm, he heard a scream come from the room next to his.

Without hesitation, he threw off the covers and raced out of his room and down the hall toward Tessa. Logan pushed opened the door to the guest room, and as it lit up with another lightning flash, Logan saw her body kicking and thrashing under the covers. Then she sat up with a start, thrusting out her arms in front of her as if defending from an attack. He watched in anguish as she screamed again, and her eyes opened to reveal a look of pain and terror. She was obviously scared of something or someone.

Logan rushed to her side and wrapped his arms around her, pulling her body in close to his. She was covered in sweat and shaking, still trapped in the horror of the dream. She sank into his chest and clung to him as if her life depended on it. A great sob raked through her body, and tears streamed onto his bare chest. Her body continued to quiver, so he pulled her onto his lap, holding her even closer.

The storm exploded around them as he continued to cradle her. Following his protective instincts, he picked her up and carried her back to his room. Logan gently lowered her into his bed and climbed in next to her, pulling the covers up to their shoulders. He could still feel her body trembling, and the tears were still falling, but he wasn't sure if she remained in the nightmare or not.

She lay with her head on his chest, tucked under his chin, and he could feel her finally start to relax as he stroked his hand through her hair. As he breathed in her scent, he noticed the pace of her breathing starting to slow and deepen as well. Finally, she succumbed to her need for rest and fell back into a deep slumber. Logan, on the other hand, couldn't have been more awake, as questions raced through his mind at a million miles an hour.

What could possibly cause this type of terror? What could have happened to break down such a tough woman, and why hadn't she mentioned it? He knew of men returning from combat and experiencing flashbacks and nightmares like this, and he wondered if she had been in a similar situation. She had told him about her injury but had been elusive as to the cause.

His eyes grew heavy as he watched her sleep. He was mesmerized by the steady rise and fall of her chest. The climax of the storm eventually passed, and all that remained was a heavy downpour with gusts of wind. He pushed aside his questions and joined Tessa in sleep now that she was safely at his side. This was just where he had wanted her in the first place—but under less stressful conditions, of course.

As Tessa slowly woke up, the first thing her mind registered was that she was lying with her head on Logan's bare chest and that his arms were around her. She was relieved to note that she still had on her clothes from last night. She wasn't sure how she'd ended up in his bed, much less in his arms. She remembered something about a dream, and someone had been holding her. She remembered hearing the storm, but that was about all.

As she raised herself up on her elbow, she looked around, seeing the blue sky out the window in front of the bed. With the storm over and the first ray of the sun shining through the window, the sky promised a clear day.

"Well, good morning, beautiful," Logan said cheerfully. Tessa snapped around to face him. He could see the confusion on her face and could feel her pulling away quickly. He kept his arm gently around her, hoping she might lie back down.

"How did I get here?" she asked.

Logan sat up and leaned back against the headboard of his bed. He was giving her the space she needed. He tugged the blanket up to his waist.

"Well, first, the storm woke me up, and then I heard you scream. I ran to your room to see what the problem was and found you in the middle of what I think was a nightmare, and you would not stop shaking and crying. You sat up screaming with your arms outstretched in front of you, so I gathered you in my arms, hoping I could get you to stop. I picked you up and carried you here to keep an eye on you and make sure the nightmare didn't come back. Besides, I like my bed a lot more than the one you were in. Anyway, I tucked you in here and held you close until you stopped shaking and crying and fell back to sleep. No funny business—I swear." He watched as different emotions played across her face, from confusion to fear to embarrassment. She tried to pull away, but Logan pulled her back.

"So, do you have these nightmares all the time? What on earth causes them?" he asked, hoping she would open up and trust him. For the first time in a long time, Tessa actually felt safe, and she considered sharing with him the source of her fear. She didn't remember Logan carrying her there or holding her until she fell asleep, but it struck her that she *had* fallen back to sleep, which had never happened before. She didn't know if she could bring herself to tell him about the dreams. She hadn't even been able to tell the doctors—or anyone, for that matter. She simply insisted she didn't remember what had happened at the warehouse. The problem was that she remembered all too vividly, but she couldn't find a way to put it into words.

To speak of it aloud would mean to relive every second of it all over again. The mere thought was unbearable. She was ashamed that he was there and had watched her in the middle of one of her episodes. She never needed anyone to lean on, and she had worked hard to be able to take care of herself no matter what. The feeling of having him hold her, protect her, and watch over her left her terribly vulnerable, needing to protect her heart. She had to get as far away from him as she could.

"I really don't want to talk about this now. I need to use the bathroom," she said, pulling away and moving off the bed. She walked into the bathroom and leaned on the door after closing it behind her. Within a few minutes, she'd mustered up the courage to face Logan again, and she opened the door to see him sitting on the bed waiting for her, wearing nothing but his boxer shorts.

"I'm sorry I took so long. I'm going to go back to my room and—"

Before she could finish her sentence, Logan was standing right in front of her. In what seemed like one long, smooth movement, he took her head in his hands, pulled her in toward his body, leaned down, and kissed her. His lips were softer than she'd imagined, and he lingered there; the kiss was long and slow, and it caught her off guard.

"I was waiting for you to come out so I could kiss you, not because I wanted you to leave. I have wanted to do that from the moment I first held you in my arms." He wrapped an arm around her shoulders, tilted her head to the side, and kissed her again. When he released her at last, she was silent and breathless, unable to speak.

"Does anything help you to sleep?" he asked.

She blinked to come to her senses. She was trying to understand what Logan asked her. When her brain came back online, she replied.

"My doctor gave me some pills, but I just do not like the way they make me feel in the morning. So, I don't take them. Sometimes if I am very tired, I do not have the nightmares. I was hoping that would be the case last night. I am so very sorry that I woke you up and that you had to see all that," she said, trying to pull away from him again. He didn't let her break away.

"Okay, so you have nightmares, and I can understand why you would not want to take the pills, but you still have not told me where they are coming from," he said.

"Please, let me go. This is something that I really cannot talk about with anyone, not even the doctors. You don't need to know any more than what I've already told you."

"I do need to know, so spill it."

Tessa could see he was not going to let her go until she told him something. She decided to say just enough to satisfy his curiosity so that they could drop the subject.

"Okay, do you remember the injury I have? Well, that's part of it. In fact, I was shot five times." She could see that he was about to ask who had shot her. "Who shot me isn't relevant here. It's a case I have been working on, but the details are privileged information. Anyway, the day I was shot, the other members of the team I work with were killed." Her voice lowered to a hushed whisper. "I was the only one to live." She again pulled away, and this time, he let her go.

Logan was shocked at hearing this. He now wanted to know more as to who had shot her and why.

Tessa walked back to her room, shut the door, and locked it. She then walked into the bathroom to take a shower. She took off her clothes and stepped into the shower, letting the hot water hit her. That was when the tears started to fall again, and with them, the sobs returned. She leaned against the wall to let the water help wash away some of the pain.

Logan walked to her room and found the door locked. He wanted and needed to talk to her more; there were questions he needed to ask. So, he walked back to his room and picked up a ring of keys to open her door. When he walked in and heard the shower going he walked to the bathroom door only to hear her crying in the shower, his heart hurt for her. He walked to the bathroom and opened the door. He watched her sitting on the floor of the shower with her legs pulled up to her chest and arms wrapped around them, crying. He grabbed a towel, turned the water off, and dropped to kneel in front of her.

"I would like to help. Let me help you, please," he said.

Tessa lifted her head and looked at him. She was tired of the pain and of living this over and over, but she did not know how to let someone help. She had always been strong, and she never leaned on anyone.

Here she was, sitting in a shower, wet and naked, with a sex god wanting to help her. It was unfair, and she felt exposed—not only her body but also her heart and soul.

"No one can help; it is just something I need to work out, so go away, please," she said.

"I could help. You just need to trust me. You are getting cold. Here let me help you up. I have a towel, and I will close my eyes," he said with a small smile. Tessa reached out for the towel, and Logan closed his eyes. She took the towel, wrapped it around her body, and tried to stand, but her legs were numb.

"Okay, I guess I will need your help to stand. At least I have the towel around me, so you can open your eyes."

As Logan helped her to stand, he caught a glimpse of some of the damage from the shots she had taken. One wound was on her leg, and another was just beneath her collarbone. Logan wrapped an arm around her to help her into the bedroom so that she could sit on the bed.

"Will you be able to get dressed by yourself now?"

"Yes, I can, and by the way, I locked the door. How did you get in?"

"My house—and I have keys to every door. Sorry, but I was worried about you and just wanted to make sure you were okay. I am going to make some coffee, and how about breakfast? The same place as yesterday?" he asked.

"Yes, that would be fine," she said, just wanting him to leave so that she could get dressed.

Tessa started to dry off and heard the doorbell ring. She stood up to get some clothes on and get ready to go. She also brushed out her hair and braided it before going downstairs.

When Tessa came out of the bedroom and down the stairs, she could smell coffee. As she turned the corner, she saw that Logan had also showered and dressed. He was standing in the kitchen with a cup of coffee, leaning on the counter while looking over some papers.

"So, who was at the door—a girlfriend I am keeping you from? Or an ex-wife maybe?" she said, pouring coffee into a cup.

"No ex or girlfriend, just someone from the office, dropping off papers for me. I work from home mostly," Logan said with a wink and a smile. "So would you care if it was a girlfriend or an ex?"

"Yes. I mean no," she said with her eyes lowered. "Well, it sounds like I am keeping you from your work, so I really should be going now that the storm is over, and I will be able to drive home safely," she said. Logan panicked. He was not ready for her to leave yet.

"No, I was going to take you to breakfast, remember? And no, you are not keeping me from my work," he said. "So, are you ready to go eat? I sure am."

Logan reached for her hand, placed it in his, and walked them out to the truck. He opened the door for her, walked around, and climbed into the truck to drive them to breakfast. The food was great, just as it had been the day before, and so was the company. Logan told her about some of the funny things that were happening with several of the businesses he owned. She thought it was ironic that he owned the bar where they'd first met. He also had a few other bars around town that he helped run.

"I really think I am keeping you from your work. We don't want you to be homeless now, right?" She laughed.

"I really do not think that a few more days will cause me to become homeless. Besides, as I told you, I work from home. There is plenty for you to keep busy with when I am working, and I really would like you to stay a few more days—or weeks or maybe forever," he said, hoping to win her over. "Besides, I really would like to get to know you better, so please stay. I have the room and the time."

Tessa looked at him with her fork halfway to her mouth and paused for a second before taking a bite. She chewed on her food slowly for a moment before answering.

"No, I think it is time I leave. I mean, I do not want to overstay my welcome, and with the way last night went, well, I really do not want to put you through that again. And it will happen again."

"Hey, I enjoy holding you and carrying you to my bed. It was no hardship on me. Besides, after you fell asleep in my arms, it was the best sleep I have had in a very long time. So, help a guy out with getting a night's sleep!" Logan said, trying to act meek.

"Something tells me if I do stay, we will not be getting much sleep," she said with a smile.

She hoped she was not making a mistake that she might not be able to recover from without more heartache.

When they were back at Logan's house, Tessa placed some calls. She made one to her mother to let her know that everything was okay and to make sure that the family was okay. Next, she called her chief to check in and see if anything had changed. Logan was in his office, working, so she walked downstairs to work on her pool skills, hoping to be able to win more games. When she was tired of that, she got a bottle of water and sat on the porch to watch the ocean. She loved the smell of the ocean air, and soon she found herself pulled toward sleep.

Logan found her sleeping in the chair. He stood watching her for a few minutes, seeing that the stress of the day was gone and watching as the wind tugged at her hair, moving it about. He walked over and lowered himself by the chair.

"Hey there, sleeping beauty. Time to get up." Logan spoke softly and gently shook her arm. He watched as her eyes slowly fluttered open and blinked a few times at him.

"Hi. Oh my, sorry. I must have fallen asleep. The sound of the waves does that to me," she said, looking at him.

"I do have better places to sleep if you still need to catch up on your beauty rest, but I, for one, think you look great the way you are," he said, smiling at her. Logan brushed a finger over her cheek, he watched as she closed her eyes and leaned into his hand.

As she started to get up, Logan moved back, stood up, and reached out to give her a hand. Tessa was still not all the way awake, and when she started to stand, one of her legs was numb and gave out. Before she could correct this, Logan had wrapped his arm around her and pulled her close to his chest.

"I like this, playing the white knight." Logan lowered his head and gently kissed her. He paused, looked into her eyes, and saw heat and longing. He picked up where they had left off, and this time, the kiss spoke of their desire and passion. Tessa moved her arm around his neck and returned the kiss with the same passion and heat, pulling him closer. Logan's other arm reached around her and pulled her even closer. His hand moved to her lower back, pulling her into his hips. She could feel how hard he was. Logan moved her head to the side, wanting a better angle. She placed her other hand on his chest.

Both of them were deep in the passion of the kiss and did not hear the front door open and close until someone coughed behind them. Logan was the first to hear the interruption and slowly pulled back. He noticed that looking into her eyes was like looking into the blue of the ocean. He smiled, ran his thumb down her cheek, kissed the tip of her nose, and pulled her close.

"Hey, Nick. Nice of you to drop by. Next time, ring the doorbell, dumbass," Logan said, looking over his shoulder to smile at the man standing in the living room.

"Sorry, bro. Did not know you had company. Would have called if I had known," Nick said, smiling and letting out a small laugh.

Tessa emerged from the fog of the kiss—and oh, what a kiss it was. She looked up to see a man just as tall and built like Logan. This man was blond and had baby-blue eyes and a smile that was warm and inviting. She pulled out of Logan's arms only to have him pull her to his side.

"Nick, this is Tessa. Tessa, this is Nick, someone who works with me."

"Nice to meet you, Nick."

"Nice to meet you too," Nick said, crossing his arms in front of his chest and smiling at them. Logan led Tessa into the great room and over to the sofa, where Tessa sat down. Logan asked if they would like a drink, and both accepted. Logan walked to a bar on the side of the great room to pull out two beers and make a drink for Tessa. He handed a beer to Nick and nodded for him to sit down. Logan sat next to Tessa and took a long pull from his beer. Nick took a drink but kept an eye on them. He knew that Logan had never before brought a woman to his home, so finding him with his arms around one, and kissing her, had surprised him. Nick could feel the heat coming off the couple. He noted that she was beautiful and had one hell of a body too.

"Okay, you can just stop now," Logan said to Nick.

"What? Not sure what you are talking about," Nick said with a smile and a wink.

"You know what I am talking about, ass. Just keep your dirty thoughts to yourself. Just saying," Logan said with a bit more attitude.

Tessa looked from one to the other and knew something was going on, but she was not sure what. Tessa excused herself to use the bathroom and freshen up, knowing that her hair probably looked as if she had walked through a wind tunnel. After she had walked upstairs and turned a corner, she could hear voices but could not make out what they were saying.

"Dude, where in the hell did you pick her up? Very nice, bro. All I can say is nice—really nice," Nick said.

For some reason Logan did not understand, that statement pissed him off. He had been pissed at Nick before but never over a woman. So, what was it about her that made him feel this way?

"Back off. She is a lady, not one of the bar women you pick up. And by the way, I would be very careful around her. She carries a gun and is highly trained in the arts. Plus, she is a marshal," Logan said before taking a pull from his beer.

Nick gave a slow whistle. "No shit. Really? And how do you know she is trained in the arts? Did she put your ass down?" He laughed. "I really wish I could have seen that. That little bit of a female dropped your ass, right?" Still laughing, he slapped his knee.

"Yes, she flipped me. Never saw it coming. She is fast and has a black belt. I also did some research on her and found out that she graduated at the top of her class, has a top mark with sniper rifles, and is an expert in most weapons. And she is the top profiler in the Southwest," Logan said, keeping an eye on the stairs. He did not want her to know he had looked her up to find out more about her and the case she was working on. When he'd read that it involved a drug cartel, he had not liked it one bit. The report stated that one of the men she'd shot was the son of the cartel's leader, Joaquin. Joaquin was not someone anyone would want to piss off, and she was the one who'd killed his son. Logan had called some of his contacts in the CIA and learned that there was much more to the story that Tessa had not shared. He'd needed to know, and now Logan was feeling uneasy about all the information he'd learned.

Tessa washed her face, touched up her makeup, and brushed and then braided her hair. Looking in the mirror, she could not get the kiss out of her head and wondered what would have happened next if his friend had not walked in. The nap had helped her feel less tired, but she was not looking forward to sleeping tonight. Turning and walking back down the hall and downstairs, she could more clearly hear their voices and bits of the conversation. As she turned the corner into the great room, she could feel Logan's eyes on her, and there was still heat in them.

"Okay, so I think that will work. Just shoot me an e-mail with the details. Bro, if you need anything else, call first, okay?"Logan said, trying to give Nick a message.

"Sure thing. No problem. Can do. Would you like me to talk to the rest of the crew about it, so they are up to speed, so to speak?" Nick asked.

"Yeah, that will be fine for now. Might need a meeting in a few days about the issues."

Tessa knew they were talking in some type of code. There was stress in both of their bodies, and their faces were hard. Tessa continued down the stairs, thinking that she was interrupting a conversation they did not want her to hear. She heard Nick say good-bye, and the front door shut.

She stood by the pool table with a ball in her hand. She gently moved it so that it would hit some of the other balls. She saw him in the corner of her eye as he walked up behind her, and she felt his arm fold around her body and pull her close to him. He bent down and rained kisses up and down her neck, first on one side and then the other. He then turned her around and, taking her in his arms, kissed her just as he had on the deck. He felt her melt in his arms. He lifted her up, and she wrapped her legs around him. He wanted to lay her down on the pool table, take off all of her clothes, and kiss each and every part of her body. Instead, he walked back toward one of the large chairs and sat down with her legs still wrapped around him.

She moved her legs so that they were next to his thighs, sitting on his lap. With one hand, Logan started to unbutton her shirt and pull it out of her jeans. Tessa pulled his T-shirt up, and they stopped kissing just long enough to pull it over his head. Then he continued kissing her, moving from her mouth down her neck and across her collarbone. With her shirt removed, he could see the swell of her breasts above her scantily red-lace bra.

Logan could see the damage from the bullet just above her right breast, but he didn't care all he wanted was to continue kissing her.

He kissed the top of her breast and pulled one breast from the cup to work his way down to her nipples. He took one in his mouth and rolled it around with his tongue. She arched her back and moaned, and Logan moved back to her lips. Just when he was ready to move to the floor, the doorbell rang, and they heard knocking on the door. Logan stopped, pulled back, and looked into her eyes. They were both breathing heavily. He lowered his head, touched her forehead with his, and let out a small laugh.

"Sorry," he said. Logan pulled back just as Tessa pushed away from him and climbed off his lap.

As she turned to pick up her shirt, she said, "Yeah, so am I." She put her shirt back on. Logan stood up, and when he could not find his shirt, he ran up the stairs to answer the door without it. He wanted to get back to her as quickly as he could. As Logan climbed the stairs, she was intrigued to see a tattoo on his left shoulder blade. The bell continued to ring until Logan opened the door. There stood both of his sisters.

"Hi. I forgot my key. Have you been working out downstairs? You're all sweaty," Jen said. She was the youngest one and was not much taller than Tessa. Jen had short blonde hair, green eyes, and a perky personality. She walked up to Logan and stood on her toes to give him a kiss on his cheek. Next to walk in was Sarah. She was the same height has Jen, but she had long black hair and green eyes. She also stood on her toes and kissed him on the cheek. Both started talking at once, but Logan was not listening. The only thing he was thinking of was how much he wanted to get back to the woman downstairs. The thought reminded him to reach down to try to adjust his jeans.

"What are you two doing here, and why didn't you call first?" Logan asked.

"We tried, but you never answer your cell, so we just drove up and hoped to catch you at home. So here we are. Surprise! Wait—you know that we are here for the celebration, right? Or did you forget again?" Jen asked. Both she and Sarah turned and looked at the stairs, realizing someone was standing there. They then both turned and looked at him with knowing smiles on their faces.

"Did not know you had company, Brother. Hi. My name is Jen, and this is my sister, Sarah," Jen said, moving toward Tessa. She reached her hand out, and Tessa shook it politely.

"My big brother here seems unable to speak. We are his little sisters. We always stay here this time of the year, and each and every time, he forgets," Sarah said, moving to shake Tessa's hand also.

"Jen, Sarah, this is Tessa Miller. Tessa, these are my sisters. As much as I love them, they are a pain in my ass most of the time."

"Nice to meet you both. Actually, I was just getting ready to leave, so please don't mind me," Tessa said as she turned to walk up the staircase. She knew it was time to leave with his family there. She did not want to stay and have to explain the nightmares that came each night or to see what might happen.

"Wait, Tessa!" Logan yelled, running up the stairs after her. When he reached her, he turned her around with both hands on her shoulders and looked into her eyes. "Hey, what is going on? You do not need to leave. I have plenty of room you know that. Plus, we still have things to talk about, and even if I'm one room short, you can bunk with me. It would not be a hardship, the way I see it." He pulled her close and kissed her forehead.

"No, I really think I should leave. They are your family, and I will just be in the way. I am going in there to pack and will be out of here in a few," Tessa said, trying to turn around to move into the bedroom. But Logan would not hear of it, so he followed her into the room and shut the door behind them.

"We are going to talk about this. Why do you think that you need to leave because my sisters are here? They come every year at this time, and yes, I forget each time. There is plenty of room, and I still would like to get to know you. I can't do that if you leave. And what about what just happened between us?" He took her head in his hands and kissed her with all the needs and wants he had for her.

"I just cannot stay, and you know why. I don't want to have to explain to them why they will hear me screaming in the middle of the night. It was bad enough when you heard it and watched it. That is one of the reasons that I live alone and will always be alone, even when I travel," she said, placing her head on his chest.

"I think I can make sure that they will not hear," he said.

"How? I have tried everything, and the only thing that has worked is drinking to the point of passing out, and I do not want to do that every day," she said, lifting her head and looking into his eyes. What Logan saw in her eyes was a woman that was troubled. She was clearly in pain from this. Which only made him want to help her that much more.

"Sleep with me—and not in the way you are thinking. When I was holding you, I could feel you relax and fall back to sleep instead of going deeper into the nightmare. So, if I am holding you all night, maybe I will be able to help stop the dreams. Besides, I am a big boy, and my sisters understand about life. So don't worry about it. I really would like you to stay. Please say yes." Logan kissed her, and when he pulled back, he ran his thumb down her cheek. He saw a war waging in her eyes, and he knew she was dealing with PSTD. It made sense after reading the report, but he wondered why the doctors had not explained it to her. Anyone who'd experienced something like she had would have nightmares. He knew many veterans came home from combat had the same thing. It was treatable; she just needs the right treatment program and some support to work through it.

"No, it's not a good idea. Please, I really should just leave. You have so much work, and now family visiting," she said with tears in her eyes. When one of the teardrops fell, Logan wiped it away with his thumb and kissed her cheek where the tear had fallen.

"No, it is a great idea! You are staying. Even if I need to keep you in my bedroom with no clothes on, you are not leaving," he said, and he pulled her close for a passionate kiss.

"Please, Logan. It will not work."

Logan pulled back to look at her and felt her tears fall on his chest.

"Yes, it will work. Just stay," he said softly. Tessa dropped her head. There was a struggle going on within her. One side wanted to stay, but the other was ready to run. Was she using the nightmares as a legitimate reason to leave, or was she afraid that the man holding her would be able to get through her walls and see into her soul? Tessa lifted her head and looked into his eyes. She reluctantly nodded and watched as his face changed. He was beaming with a smile so bright that she felt the need to look away.

"You won't regret this. I promise. How about you grab your bags and move over to my room? I am going to put a shirt on and talk to my sisters, and I think we should go out. I know of a great place," Logan said, and then he gave her a quick kiss. Logan walked back to his room, grabbed a T-shirt, and quickly put it on as he went downstairs to have a talk with his sisters.

Jen asked Sarah, "Do you think something is going on? I mean, he has never had a woman here. He is the love-them-and-leave-them type, right?"

Sarah just looked at her, shaking her head. "Jen, he is a big boy, and if he wants to have her here, why not? Besides, it is time for him to find someone. He has been alone a long time. He deserves to find happiness, and if she is the right one, I think it's great," Sarah said.

Logan heard that and smiled, liking that at least Sarah was on his side. And yes, Tessa was the one. He could feel it with every cell in his body. Now he had to figure out how to get Tessa to feel the same and stop running.

"Okay, now that you are here and see I have a guest, just let me explain a few things. First, she is staying with me in my room. No questions or remarks about this—get it?" he looked at each one and then continued. "Next, she is a deputy US marshal, and she does carry a gun and a badge. So, when you see the gun, do not freak out. Lastly, she is on medical leave because she was hurt in her last case. Do not ask her to talk about it. Got it?" Logan said, giving them both a look that said he meant business.

"Yeah, sure, no problem," they both said.

"So, she really is a marshal? That is so cool," Jen said, smiling, and Logan could see the wheels turning as to all the things she wanted to ask Tessa.

"Jen, remember what I said—no questions. I mean it," Logan said. "Sarah, could you call into that restaurant that we all like and get a table for, say, about seven or so? You know which one—it's on the bay," Logan said.

"Sure, I know which one. Can I go to my room now? I need to unpack and make some calls."

"Yes, she was in the guest room on the ocean side, but both of the rooms that you usually use are good to go," Logan said as he walked into his office.

CHAPTER 6

TESSA PACKED UP AND MOVED NEXT door. After dropping her bag, she sat on the bed.

"What the hell am I doing? I don't see this turning out well," she said aloud to herself. She then decided to make the bed, pick up a few things around the room, and put the dirty clothes in the laundry basket. She walked downstairs, but not seeing anyone; she went into the kitchen to clean up. She was trying to keep busy for the time being, not knowing what to do with herself now. After cleaning up the kitchen and walking back into the great room, she heard typing, so she turned and walked toward Logan's office, which looked like an office that she might find in an office building.

"All you need is a secretary out front to take calls," she said, leaning against the doorframe.

"Well, I do have an opening. Would you like to apply?" he said with a smile, patting his lap for her to sit. Tessa walked over but thought better of it. She shook her head at him and continued to walk around the room. She stopped in front of a large map with lights on it.

"What's with the map?" she said, looking over her shoulder at him. She remembered him telling her that he owned several businesses and judging by this map; he had many all over the world. Logan stood, walked over, and leaned a hip on the desk against the wall by the map.

"The green lights are the ones I own and are part of the family business that I took over when my father passed away. The yellow lights are businesses that I have an interest in, but not a controlling one. The red ones are those that are problems and need to have some work done to make them profitable again," he said.

Tessa turned and looked at him, wondering who exactly this man was. Logan returned to his desk and sat down to continue with his work on the computer. As Tessa walked around looking at the many maps and works of art, she could feel his eyes follow her around the room.

"So, this place we are going to—will I need to dress up?"

"No, not really. I just do not like to wait for a table, and they know me there and will be happy to have the table ready for us when we need it," he said, looking up. He folded his arms across his chest and leaned back in his chair.

"So, what are you thinking so hard about over there?" he asked.

Tessa stopped and turned around, not sure if she wanted him to know what she was thinking.

"Oh, just that you have a lot of great artwork here," she said, looking at him from under her lashes. Then she walked out of the room and downstairs. She did not want him to know how much he rattled her. She still did not think it was a good idea for her to stay, even if he believed he could keep the demons away from her dreams.

Logan continued to sit there. For some reason, he knew that what she'd told him was not the truth. However, he also knew he could get the truth from her one way or another. He sat up and continued writing an e-mail to a friend who worked at the CIA, requesting to be kept updated on the information he had asked about. He finished the e-mail, sent it, and closed the computer. He walked out to the great room to look for Tessa. Logan walked upstairs to his bedroom, still looking for her, but when he couldn't find her, he walked out to the hall again and almost ran over Sarah.

"Sorry. Have you seen Tessa? Wanted to see if she would like a drink before we go. Did you get a hold of the restaurant so that the table will be ready?"

"Yes, I called, and the table will be ready, and no, I have not seen her. Have you looked downstairs? She might be there."

Logan jogged downstairs. When he walked into the basement, he looked around and still did not see her. Logan put his hands on his hips, starting to get worried when he spotted the door opened to the outside patio. He walked to it and looked out to see Tessa standing there. Her arms were wrapped around her sides, and her hair was free and blowing in the wind. She was looking out to sea.

"There is a better view upstairs," he said, and he walked up behind her, wrapped his arms around her, and kissed her neck.

"Do you want a drink before we leave for dinner?" he asked, continuing to kiss her neck.

"What are you doing?" she said, turning around in his arms.

Logan wrapped his arms around her and pulled her close. "If I need to tell you, then I guess I am not doing it right," he said, and he pulled back to look into her eyes. What he saw confused him, and he pulled back more, placing his hands on her upper arms.

"Okay, so what is going on inside this head of yours?" he asked, pointing to her head. "I do not think it has to do with the garden out here," he said, looking down at her.

She turned to continue to look out at the ocean, not sure herself what she was thinking or if she wanted to tell him. "Nothing, just enjoying the view, but I could use that drink," she said, looking up at him with a smile.

Logan knew she was not telling him the truth, but for now, he was not going to push for her to answer him. Instead, he was going to wait and see if she would open up on her own.

"Sure, come on. Let's get you that drink so we can go eat. I do not know about you, but I am hungry, and I can hear a steak calling my name," Logan said with a smile. Logan turned, taking her hand, and walked her back into the basement. He locked the door and walked up the stairs to the great room to get her a drink. He hoped it might help her to talk to him. If not, maybe she'd tell him later what was going on and what she was thinking about, when she was wrapped in his arms and relaxed.

Dinner was great. She loved seafood, and Logan was not kidding when he told her that the food there was the best on the coast. She enjoyed a few glasses of wine and was entertained by the conversation between Logan and his sisters. She was even able to laugh at some of the things his sisters told her about him growing up.

"Hey, it is not fair—three against one! And why are you guys bringing up all the embarrassing things about me? You know there are a lot of things

I have on both of you," Logan said, pointing his finger at Jen and Sarah and smiling.

"Yeah, yeah, but it is so fun to see you wiggle knowing we have all this dirt on you and are sharing it with Tessa! Besides, she needs to know this stuff so she can have something to hold over you later on," Jen said, laughing.

Tessa just smiled and took a sip of her wine, thinking that for the first time in a long time, she did not have her walls up and was having a great evening. She could not remember the last time she'd had this much fun. Logan looked over at her and noticed a far-off look on her face as if she were thinking of something. But by the smile on her face, he figured it was something good.

"So, what are you thinking now?" he asked, leaning over close to her ear so that his sisters would not hear. Tessa turned to look into his eyes, she was only an inch from his lips and could have kissed him, but instead, she just smiled.

"That I am having a wonderful time and cannot remember the last time I had," she said. Logan moved closer and kissed her softly, and as he pulled back to look into her eyes, he smiled.

"Good. That was the plan—to wine and dine you and get you to relax," he said, raising his eyebrow a few times and then winking at her before sitting back. Logan paid for the dinner and thanked the restaurant staff for the great food. He opened the door for his sisters to walk out first. When Tessa started to walk out the door, Logan took her hand, placed a kiss on it, and then laced their fingers together as they walked out to the car.

After getting home and making sure the door was locked, Logan's sisters said good night and retired to their rooms. Logan found Tessa out on the deck, listening to the ocean, her arms wrapped around herself. He could tell she was cold, so he walked up and wrapped himself around her. He could feel her slightly shivering. He placed his chin on top of her head and pulled her close. She seemed to fit him like a glove.

"I missed the ocean, living in Phoenix. There is something calming that pulls me toward it. I could stay here forever and listen to it," she said as she continued to stand there and listen to the waves.

"I am sure you could, but I think you might need to put on a coat. It is cold out here." He kissed the top of her head, tightening his arms around her and pulling her closer to warm her body. "I think it is time to come in; it is getting late," he said as he turned her around in his arms. She looked up at him, and at the same time, he lowered his head and kissed her. There was a great deal of heat in the kiss, and she melted against him as he wrapped his arms around her. They stood there for a moment, kissing, embracing, and enjoying each other. Logan pulled back and kissed the tip of her nose. He could feel her heart racing as much as his was.

"I think we should take this inside and upstairs," he said before placing a quick kiss on her lips. He took her hand, walked back into the room, closed the door, and made sure it was locked.

"I need to make sure that all the doors and windows are locked before I turn on the alarm system. I will meet you upstairs," he said, taking her hand and placing a kiss on it. He then turned to walk downstairs.

Tessa walked up to Logan's bedroom. She kept thinking that she did not want to wake up his sisters with one of her nightmares. She walked into the bedroom and grabbed some clothes before walking to the bathroom. The wine and dinner had her feeling relaxed, and she hoped a hot bath would help to relax her more. After filling up the tub and taking off her clothes, she stepped into the tub and slowly lowered her body. She loved feeling the bite of the hot water tingle across her skin. She sank all the way down, leaned back, took a deep breath, and felt her muscles relaxing. Logan walked into the bedroom to find it empty and then saw that the bathroom light was on. He shut the bedroom door and walked toward the bathroom.

"Tessa, are you okay?" he said just before he pushed the door open. What he saw made his tongue drop out of his mouth. There was the woman he had been dreaming of, lying back in a tub filled with bubbles. She was covered all the way up to her chin. She sat with her head back and eyes closed. She had one knee up and a hand on the side of the tub. Logan knelt down next to the tub, took her hand, and placed a kiss on it.

"Is there room for one more in there?"

Tessa smiled and opened one eye to look at him. "No, I was just about ready to get out. But I won't drain the water if you would like to enjoy it after I am out," she teased.

"It would not be the same without you," he said, smiling back at her.

"I could use a towel now. Could you hand one to me, please?" she asked. Logan reached behind him for the towel and held it up for her to step into before wrapping it around her and kissing her. Tessa pulled back and looked up into his eyes. What she saw took her breath away. His eyes shone with love, desire, passion, and heat. She wondered how this gorgeous man could look at her this way, knowing how damaged she was.

"I do not know if I can do this; it has been a very long time for me," she said, still looking at him. She needed him to understand that she desired nothing more right now than to make love to him, but at the same time, she was scared. Thoughts raced through her mind. How could she face armed men without blinking an eye but be too afraid to show her most inner self to this man? He had only shown her kindness and understanding. He was strong enough to help her through the one part of her life she had no control over but gentle enough to look at her with loving eyes.

"We will not do anything until you are ready. But I just want you to know that when the time does come, and it sure as hell will, I'll be ready. And, babe, I am going to rock your world—you can fucking bet on it!" he said before kissing her senseless again. Logan stepped back and gave her space to get dressed in an effort to control his lust. Tessa watched him move out of the room and then closed the door behind him. She turned to dry off and got dressed in the oversized T-shirt she always wore to bed. She brushed her hair and teeth before coming out of the bathroom. Logan was standing in front of the window, looking outside but not really seeing anything. He was so deep in thought that he did not notice her approaching until she touched his arm. Logan turned and looked down. She could have been wearing rags, and they would not have taken away from her beauty. He leaned down and placed a kiss on her lips.

"I need to take a shower; make yourself comfortable," he said, and he walked into the bathroom and shut the door. A moment later, she heard the shower turn on. She walked over to the bed, pulled the covers down, and crawled in. As she lay down, she pulled the covers over her body and felt the pull of sleep.

Logan took a long time in the shower. The lust he was feeling for Tessa had made him hard, and he needed to take care of it before he crawled into bed and layed next to her. Logan finished up, pulled on some cotton pants, and turn off the light. He walked into the bedroom to find that she had crawled into bed and was fast asleep. Her breathing was slow and steady. She was lying on her left side, facing the edge of the bed. He walked to the other side, turned on the security system, and shut off the light. He slid under the covers next to her, put one arm under her head, and, with the other, reached over to pull her closer. She moaned and whimpered slightly as her body moved closer to his. He placed his lips close to her ear and whispered softly, "Let me in, I can take care of the demons. I love you," He then kissed her neck and lay back down to go to sleep.

In the early morning hours, Logan began to wake up, confused by the sound of someone crying. The sensation of someone moving next to him fully awakened him. He opened his eyes just before the cry turned to a sob, and he realized Tessa was beginning to have a nightmare. He heard her cry out several times, and she moved restlessly. Logan wrapped his arms around her and softly repeated in her ear that she was okay, he was with her, and no one would hurt her. He slowly rocked her and whispered to her until her heart rate slowed and she calmed down, returning to a peaceful sleep. He continued to hold her close as he fell asleep again.

When he woke up hours later, the bed next to him was empty and cold. He sat up and quickly got out of bed. Seeing that the bathroom was dark, he walked downstairs. The smell of coffee hit him before he reached the bottom of the stairs. He looked around the kitchen and then the great room, but he still did not find her. He was ready to go down to the bottom floor, when something in the corner of his eye caught his attention. He looked out at the deck to see her sitting in one of the chairs with a blanket wrapped around her, looking out to the ocean. He walked back to the kitchen to get a cup of coffee and then to the hall closet to grab a coat. He walked out to the deck and stood next to her before he sat down. He leaned over and kissed her on the side of her neck.

"Good morning, beautiful," he said as he settled in to enjoy the view with her. The morning was a bit foggy and cold, so he was glad she had a blanket around her since she was still wearing just her nightshirt. They sipped their coffee and watched as someone walked along the beach with a dog.

"How are you doing? Did you sleep okay?" he said, turning to face her.

"Yes, I did. It was strange; it seemed like I was going into a dream, and when it started getting bad, all I heard was your voice. You were telling me over, and over that I was safe, and no one would hurt me, because you were there to protect me and keep me safe, because it was your job," she said while looking at him.

Logan smiled and took a sip of coffee. "Yes, you did start to have a nightmare early this morning, and yes, I did tell you those things. And lo and behold, you settled down and fell back to sleep," he told her.

Tessa admitted that he'd been right. Just being held by him did help with the nightmares. In fact, it was the first good night's sleep she'd had in a long time.

"Thank you for what you did; it helped me more than I thought it would. But I am sorry that I woke you up, so I'm glad that you were able to go back to sleep," she said, dropping her eyes. She took a sip of her coffee.

With a wink and a smile, he replied, "Hey, the pleasure was all mine. I enjoyed holding you against me all night. Would like to do more—"

Just then, Jen stuck her head out the door and said she couldn't find anything to make for breakfast. She asked if anyone wanted to go out to eat instead. They agreed and decided to get dressed and ready to go.

A couple hours had passed by the time they were done eating. Sarah reminded Logan that they needed to get ready for their busy schedule of activities. Part of the reason they visited each year was to volunteer for an annual celebration. Each sister was part of a different committee, and their tasks kept them busy during their stay with Logan. They returned to the house, and the girls disappeared to their rooms.

Tessa's phone rang as she walked into the house. She looked at the number and immediately answered. "Hi, Mom. What's going on?" She smiled into the phone, but her smile quickly faded. Her mouth tightened, and she looked pissed, occasionally saying, "Hmm," or "Yeah." When she lifted her eyes to look at Logan, what he saw caused him to take a step forward. Her dark blue eyes were hard; there was nothing soft or loving about them.

"Okay. Yes, I understand, and I will be there in about an hour or so. Just keep the doors locked, and if he tries to get in, call 911. Do you understand me, Mom? Do not let him in!" she said, nearly snarling. She closed her phone and took a deep breath to calm her rage before she spoke.

"I have a family problem I need to take care of, and I need to leave now. Thank you for all of your help and for letting me stay here," she said, taking a step forward. "It's important that I get to my mom as quickly as possible."

"Can I help? It sounds like you could use some," he said, looking at her. He didn't want her to leave. He knew the danger she could be in, and his first thought was that her family was being targeted by the cartel.

"No, I think I can take care of it. Like I said, it is a family problem, and they need me there to help. Again, thank you, but I need to get packed and go," she said, trying to move around him toward the house.

Logan stepped in front of her to stop her from entering the house. He needed to go along to make sure she was safe. He wanted to honor the promise he'd made to her last night just before he fell asleep: *"Let me in, I can take care of the demons. I love you,"*

He did not know if she'd heard him. Plus, she was unaware of the dangers that she was in that he found as he had probed about behind her back. He needed to come up with an excuse to follow her and be there to help if need be.

"Okay, stop by my office before you go. I have a few calls to make and would like to say goodbye to you in my own special way before you go," he said as he rubbed his thumb down the side of her face. They both walked into the house; she headed upstairs, while he went to the office. He closed the door and pulled out his phone.

"Nick, we have a problem," he said into the phone.

Tessa packed up her things and carried her bag downstairs. She placed it by the front door and then walked to the office door and knocked. Logan responded, and she opened the door to find him talking on the phone and typing on the computer.

"Yes, that is what I said. The meeting is set, and I will need to be there, so go ahead and get me the information. Send it to me by e-mail and call me when you have everything ready." He tapped his finger on the screen for the call to end.

"Is everything all right? You sound upset," she said. She watched as he stood and walked around the desk toward her. When he stood right in front of her, he placed his hands on her face and lowered his head. He kissed her slowly at first and then wrapped one arm around her, pulling her closer and making the kiss deeper. She melted into him and wrapped her arms around him. She could feel the hard muscles of his abs and the muscles of his back. He backed her up to the door and covered her body with his.

"I need to go," she said between kisses, and she tried to clear her brain of the lust he'd inspired. All she could think was *Damn; he is a great kisser!* She pushed at him to step back and looked up at his green eyes. They were both breathing hard, and their hearts were racing.

"I know, but I also know that I cannot live without you. Just the thought of not being with you makes me crazy," he said as he lowered his forehead to rest on hers. He placed his hands on the door by her head, trying to get some type of control over his body. "I just received a call that I need to go to Salem about a deal that is not going well. They will only talk to me about it, so I guess if I have to go there as well, how about I ride along with you? That way, when you are done and free, you can drive me back, and we can enjoy more time together here." He swept his hand toward the window that looked out onto the ocean.

"Logan, I have no idea how long I am going to be, or if I will be able to come back here. So, I really do not think that is a good idea. Besides, where would you stay? And you would have no way around without a car. I am going to be very busy with my family thing," she said, looking up at him.

"I can rent a car, and they do have hotels there. I was hoping we could share a room," he said, nipping her ear.

"I need to leave right now, and you would need to pack. I have no time to wait," she said, trying hard not to moan.

"Hey, I can be done in five minutes. You can wait five minutes, right?" he said, drawing her lips to his. Tessa just nodded, and Logan moved to open the door and then raced upstairs to pack.

"What the hell am I doing? This is not a good idea, not one damn bit," she said to herself. She heard him call for his sisters to tell them he was going out of town. He reminded them to make sure to lock and arm the house and to call him on his cell if they needed him. Logan walked down the stairs toward the front door, where she was waiting. He reached down to pick up her bag and opened the door for her, and they walked to her car. She opened the trunk so that Logan could place their bags inside, and then she unlocked the doors and climbed in to start the car.

"I will let you know that what I am going to be doing is really not that ethical, but I need to so that I can get there quickly," she said as she turned the key, and the car roared to life. She backed out of the driveway and drove down the lane toward the highway. Once she was on the highway, she turned the lights on, and when there was traffic in the way, she turned on the siren to get the vehicles out of the way. She flew down the highway, going well over the speed limit, and he was impressed with the way she handled the car. They passed a state cop, and soon the cop was right behind them with his lights on. Tessa said a few unladylike words and then pulled over, getting her information out and ready.

"Driver step out of the car with your hands up, passenger step out with your hands up, too," the officer said, standing behind the open door of his car.

"Shit, I really do not have time for this bullshit. Make sure your hands are in plain sight at all times," she told Logan. She opened the door slowly and raised her hands. Then she got out of the car, turned her back to the officer, and walked backward, as instructed until she was told to stop. Logan also was walking backward with his hands up as the other officer reached for him. The officer placed one of the cuffs on her right wrist, twisted behind her, and lowered her left hand to her back. He cuffed it and turned her around, and the first thing he saw was her gun, followed by the badge on her belt. The officer then looked up and back down again at the badge.

"Are you an officer?" he asked, looking at her.

"Yes, I am an officer. My ID is in my coat pocket on the right side," she told him, and the officer reached into her pocket to get her ID. After looking at it and calling it in, he returned to uncuff her and return her ID.

"Sorry for this, but we really do not get many cars with lights like those around here."

"I understand, and there is no need to apologize," she said, taking her ID from him. She turned, walked back to her car, Logan was already sitting in the car as she started it, and drove off.

"We are okay. I am hoping that they have called this in, so if we come across more of them, they will not stop me. I need to get there like now."

It took only forty-five minutes to get there, and when she pulled into the driveway of her parents' house, she told him to stay there. She jumped out of the car, ran up to the house, and knocked on the door. When the door opened, a woman grabbed her and hugged her. They talked for a bit, and Tessa walked back to the car as the woman shut the door.

"Okay, so now that I am here and all is okay, I guess we should try to find someplace to stay." She started the car and backed out of the driveway. As she'd been talking to her mom, he'd made some calls, found a place, and made arrangements. Logan wanted to pay for the room because he'd asked for a suite.

After they dropped off their bags, they needed to find someplace to eat. Afterward, when they got back to the hotel, Logan said he had some calls to make and e-mails to return. He told her he'd wanted the suite because he might need to work late and did not want to disturb her when she was sleeping. When they entered the room, she saw a large fruit basket, a few bottles of champagne, and several vases of flowers. She turned to look at him, and he wrapped an arm around her, pulled her close, and kissed her until her toes curled. He set her down on her feet and slapped her ass as he walked around her to set up his computer and briefcase. He pulled out his phone and started to make calls, no longer looking at her. Tessa walked into the bedroom to unpack and take a shower. After putting on the oversized T-shirt she always wore, she brushed her teeth and combed out her hair. She looked out into the living room to see Logan still on the phone and computer, so she decided to turn down the bed and crawl in. She punched the pillow a few times and tried to go to sleep. It took a bit, but after several minutes, she could feel sleep pull her under.

Logan heard the shower turn off and kept the conversation going with as few words on his part as necessary. He was listening for her to walk out of the bedroom and say good night. When she never came out, Logan walked over to the door, opened it, and looked in to see her sleeping on her side. He walked back to the table he had set up as a desk and continued to talk to Nick.

"She is asleep now. So, do you have anything else? I am not happy with what you were able to get. I really think there is something going on that is not being reported. That asshole is up to something; I feel it. I need you to dig around and see if you can find out more," he said. He had a feeling deep inside of him that something was going on, and he was going to get to the bottom of it. Logan closed the computer, checked the door to make sure it was locked and turned out the lights. He needed to take a shower, as he was not yet ready for bed.

He stood in the shower for a long time, thinking about the information he'd obtained. When he stepped out of the shower and dried off, he was ready for bed. He decided not to wear anything to bed, which was normal for him. After crawling into bed and turning out the lights, he moved closer to Tessa and wrapped his arms around her. He pulled her close, kissed her on her ear, and whispered, "Let me in, I can take care of the demons. I love you and will always want you. Come hell or high water; I'll make sure you are safe." He fell asleep knowing she was only safe when she was with him.

When he woke up, he saw light coming through the drapes. He felt that she was not next to him, but the bed was still a bit warm as if she'd just left. Logan crawled out of bed and stretched his neck back and forth. He reached for his jeans to pull them on before walking out into the living room to find her. Tessa was sitting at the table, drinking coffee and reading the paper. She felt him before she saw him, as he came up behind her and kissed her on the back of her head.

"Good morning, sweetheart. Did you sleep well? I did not notice if you have a bad dream."

"Hi, handsome, and yes, I did. It's strange, but I did not dream last night for the first time in months." She smiled up at him. Logan bent down and kissed her before pouring a cup of coffee and sitting down beside her.

"So, what is going on today?" she asked. "You worked late last night. I did not feel you come to bed."

"Not that late, maybe an hour or so after you went to bed. I have a meeting this morning at ten. I am going to rent a car, so I can get around. That should free you up to do what you need to do." He took a sip of coffee and smiled that wicked smile.

She knew he was up to something. She wasn't sure if she believed his story regarding why he was there, but for now, she decided to play along and see what happened next. She needed to go see her mom and find out what was going on and what she needed to do to fix it.

CHAPTER 7

TESSA DROVE TO HER PARENTS' HOUSE, hoping for the best but preparing for the worst. She walked up to the door and knocked. When the door opened, she stepped in and gave her mom a hug. Then she saw that her mother had a black eye.

"Why didn't you call me? And do not fucking tell me you ran into a door!" She was so mad that she could not stop shaking. She walked into the house, where a few chairs and things were broken, and the back door was broken in. Tessa knew she needed to get control of her emotions, because the way she was feeling, she might do something she would later regret. She stood there looking around, trying to control her breathing. She needed to go to that place inside where she could think logically and make plans to stop this and keep her mom and brothers safe.

"Why, Mom? Why didn't you call me? I told you to call if he came back and to call 911. At least tell me you called 911 and he is in jail over this." She waited for her mom to answer, and when her mom did not say anything, Tessa turned around. Her mom was looking at her feet.

"Mom, you did call 911, right?" When her mom still did not answer but continued to look down at her feet, Tessa closed her eyes and threw her head back. She was having trouble getting her anger under control.

"You did not call. So where is he now?" she said, looking at her mom. "I need to know so I can get him and arrest him for all of this." She waved her arms around and pointed at her mom.

"I do not know. I was knocked out, and when I came to, he was gone, along with some of his things from the other room," she said, pointing to the room where her father kept all of his hunting stuff. Tessa walked in and saw that the gun cabinet, which was usually locked at all times, was wide open, revealing which guns were missing. She looked into the closet and saw that some of her father's camping supplies were missing. She knew he thought he'd been born in the wrong time and thought of himself as a mountain man. She also knew which way he might have gone because they did a lot of camping and hunting in the area. If she could find out where he had driven to, she could track him. She turned around and almost knocked her mom over. She stepped around her and walked quickly out to her car. She carried her own guns in a special place hidden in the trunk of her car. She opened the trunk to see what she had and to make a list of things she would need to get. Tessa turned back to her mom, who was now standing out on the porch.

"He is running, and I know right about where I can find him. I will bring him in. Do you have anyone to stay with? Because this house is not safe to stay in. Until you can get the door fixed," she said, and her mom nodded in reply. "Good. Pack what you need, call someone to fix the back door, and then let me know where you will be. I will let you know what is going on. It is okay, Mom. Trust me; I know what I am doing. I will be okay," she said, getting into her car. She had her rifle and knives but needed some gear. She drove to a sporting goods store to buy the gear she'd need to find her father and bring him back. She found everything she needed but still had a few things back at the hotel that she would need also. She hoped Logan was not there to stop her.

*   *   *

Logan met with Nick at a local Starbucks to discuss everything Nick had found out. The information was not good. Logan had suspected that a contract was out on Tessa for the murder of the drug cartel's son, and the information that Nick had been able to get confirmed it.

"So, do you know who is coming after her? Because I was unable to get that information from my sources or from the ones you gave me. I do not understand why in the fuck they have not let her know. If she is out walking around, she could be killed. She may need to go into hiding," Nick said, taking a drink of his coffee.

Logan was thinking the same thing and was trying to come up with a plan to take her someplace to keep her safe.

"I know that if her superiors have the same information, the fuckers should at least let her know. By not letting her know, they are putting her life in danger, and I will not stand here and let that happen. We need to come up with a plan to get her someplace safe and also find out who it is that has the contract on her," Logan said, annoyed.

"See if you can find someplace where we can go until this all blows over," he said to Nick as they both stood up and walked to the door. Logan turned and gave Nick a nod and then walked to his rental car. He headed back to the hotel, hoping Tessa was there so that he wouldn't need to go after her.

*   *   *

Tessa was on the road in a rented truck with her backpack loaded and her rifle and guns next to her on the seat. She was going to find her father and bring him back. She had to make this right for her mom. She'd left a note for Logan back in the suite, telling him she was going to be gone and didn't know for how long. She suggested it might be best for him to go back home and said she would let him know when she got back.

*   *   *

Logan walked into the room and looked around but did not find Tessa. When he walked to the desk, he spotted the note she'd left. Logan read and then reread the note, and each time, he grew more pissed. Logan pulled his phone from his back pocket and hit a number. Before long, Nick was on the line.

"We have a problem. She is not here. Something about needing to take care of a problem," he said after a moment. Then he yelled into the phone, "No, I do not know where the fuck she is! Do a trace on her phone and tell me where the hell she is! And do it like yesterday!" He threw the phone and heard it break apart. "Fuck!" He walked into the bedroom to find that all of her stuff was missing. He knew she was going to see her mom, so that was where he headed, hoping to find some answers.

He arrived at her mom's house and parked behind a car, where he spotted her mom putting a bag in the trunk. She stood up and turned toward him as he walked up to her. The first thing he noticed was the black eye.

"Hello. I am a friend of Tessa's. My name is Logan, and I wanted to know if you know where she is. She and I were to meet up for lunch when I received a text that she was going out of town. Do you know where?" he said, using his charm and a great big smile.

"Not really sure, but I think I know the area she might be going to. But you are going to find it hard to get to her. You see, she is tracking her father. He is on the run and took some of his guns and camping stuff. I think they're in the same area where they did their deer hunting and camping. It is in the Coast Mountains," she said, pointing toward the west. Logan looked in the direction she was pointing.

"I'm sorry, but I really do not understand. You mean a cabin in the mountains?" he asked, confused.

"No cabin, just the mountains. She is going to track him down and bring him back," she said.

Logan was not sure why she would do that or if she would be able to track him and bring him back. "How can she do that? What I mean is, even if she finds him, how will she get him back here?"

"She was raised hunting and camping in those woods. She knows them. Plus, she has had training in that field and is one of the best at tracking someone," her mom said with a great deal of pride in her voice.

"Okay, and thank you for the information," he said. He turned, walked back to his car, pulled his backup phone from his pocket, and hit a number.

"Have you got a lock on her yet? I know which way she went, just not sure exactly where" he said.

"Yes, I have a lock, and she is on the move. Must be in a vehicle; she is flying, from what I have on my screen," Nick said.

Logan closed the screen and drove out of the driveway and down the street to meet up with Nick to see about a plan to find her before someone else did.

CHAPTER 8

TESSA KNEW SHE WAS IN THE right area, but she was having trouble with some of the different roads because it had been a long time since she had been up there. Much of the area had changed: trees had been cut down, and landmarks had been removed. But she was tracking him with her instincts. She somehow could feel a pull to the left as she came to a fork in the road. She drove several miles until she reached a large open area and pulled over.

She reached for her binoculars and slowly scoped the hillside and the road on the other side of the canyon. As she was just about to stop, she spotted a truck that looked like her father's. Tessa followed the road until she came across the truck. She grabbed her gun and stepped out. She looked all around, slowly walked up to the truck, and placed one hand on the hood. It was cold. She returned to the rental truck and grabbed her backpack and weapons before locking it. She strapped a gun to her hip, placed the knife holder on her belt loop, and walked into the area, looking for his trail.

Logan and Nick were closing in on the spot where she had stopped. As they watched the screen, the blinking light showed that she was moving slower now, which could mean she was walking. They continued on to find the area where she'd left the truck and taken off into the woods. They both saw a vehicle behind them, and each time they stopped, the trailing vehicle would also stop. Each man looked at the vehicle and knew they were being followed, which meant there was a threat to Tessa close by.

They had no idea which way Tessa was going or if she would come across her pursuers. After several miles, Logan spotted two trucks sitting along the side of the road. After getting out, Logan checked both and found that one was still warm on the hood; the other one was cold. Both Logan and Nick grabbed their equipment from the back of the truck, checked their weapons, put on their backpacks, and holstered their guns and knives. They only carried their handguns.

Nick still had a signal on Tessa from her cell phone. Logan used hand signals to tell Nick they should move to the side and take different trails to find which way she had gone. It only took a moment for Nick to find the way, and he signaled to Logan. As they quickly followed the trail, Logan heard a vehicle pull up slowly near the spot where they had parked their truck. He signaled to Nick to get off the path and move parallel to the trail. They had to keep out of sight until they knew who seemed to be following them.

Tessa followed the trail, stepping carefully and looking for false trail leads or traps that might have been set. She would stop and listen every few hundred feet. A few times, she thought she heard something, and she pulled her rifle around to the front and clipped it onto her belt. She was wearing fingerless gloves and army-issue boots. She knew these woods, and she had taken several training classes on tracking and survival. This was where she felt most comfortable. She could tune in to the sounds and smells of the woods. She knew that over to her left was a deer; she couldn't see it, but she could smell it.

Tessa continued to walk slowly, checking to make sure she still had the trail of her father. When a smell that she knew hit her, she stopped and knelt down, looking around her and knowing he was close. Tessa was wearing an old coat she kept in a bag. The coat had been around horses, so no one would be able to smell her. She checked the wind's direction to stay downwind and continued on, keeping low and quiet. After coming around a small hill and through some heavy brush, she could see some smoke and what looked like a cave in the hillside. She continued to move slowly toward the cave opening, staying to the right of it in case someone was watching. Tessa heard a cough. She stopped, lowered herself, and waited, watching to see if she had been spotted.

A man stepped out of the cave. He had a rifle and looked around. He turned his head as if to listen better and then pointed the rifle into the trees and looked through the scope. After a few moments, he dropped his rifle down and walked back into the cave. Tessa crawled closer to the mouth of the cave, staying to the right in case he walked back out. When she was almost to the mouth, she heard a sound in the direction from which she had come. Slipping back into the trees to stay hidden and to watch who might be there, she could see two men about ten yards apart, slowly coming toward the cave. The man stepped out of the cave with his rifle in his hand, pointing it toward the sounds of the two men.

"I do not know who the hell you are, but you can just go back the way you came," he said.

Tessa had backed into the trees and blended into them. She stayed quiet and still, watching and waiting. Logan stepped out of the woods, followed by Nick. They both saw that the man had a rifle pointed at them. Tessa recognized Logan and Nick and knew she needed to do something to control this situation before someone got hurt. She slowly stepped out of the trees and stood at the man's back. Logan and Nick saw her as she slipped out of the trees behind the man.

"Drop the rifle, Dad. Do not make me shoot you," she said with her gun pointed at his back. She did not think he would give up that easily and was prepared for a fight. He moved to swing at her, but she sides stepped, and she had her gun pointed right at him as he came all the way around. What he saw was her gun pointing to his forehead, a sight that gave his heart a skip. With her other hand, she grabbed the rifle and took it from him. Her hand holding the gun never wavered, and the look in her eyes was cold and deadly. This was what bad guys saw when they were face-to-face with her before she cuffed and arrested them.

"Now, hands above your head, and lace your fingers," she said, and when he did not move, she said in a tone that dripped with ice and fury, "Now! I will not tell you again! You will be on the ground, eating dirt." She never looked away or moved as her father placed his hands on his head. The look he gave her was one of fury as he did as he was told.

"Now get on your knees, and cross your legs," she said. He slowly lowered to the ground and did as she said. Not once did she move or take her eyes off of him. Tessa grabbed her cuffs and cuffed his hands together.

"Now get up," she told him. There was strength in her words. She was digging deep to try to treat him as if he were any other criminal and not her dad. She walked over to him and patted him down, taking the guns and knives he had on him, before having him sit down on the ground.

"How in the hell did you find me, Daughter?" he asked.

"Easy—I tracked you. A blind person could have found you, as you did not try to hide it one bit, old man. And besides, I was trained for this," she said.

"This is your dad? Why? I mean, why would you come after him?" Logan asked.

Tessa looked at Logan, trying to understand why he was there and how in the fuck he'd found her. "What in the hell are you doing here? How did you find me?" she said, not pleased one damn bit that they were there.

"We really do not have time for this. There are some very unpleasant people right behind us, and they're moving in fast," Nick said, looking behind him. Tessa looked behind him to see if she could see anyone. She saw only trees, and because the pursuers were downwind, she would not be able to smell anyone coming.

"Who are they, and why the hell are they here?" she said, looking first at Nick and then at Logan. She continued to look first at one and then the other, and when they did not talk, she became pissed.

"I am just about ten seconds from going nuclear, so one of you had better start talking, or I swear to god it's not going to be pretty when I get done! Now, talk!" she shouted. Logan looked at Nick as if they were silently talking without words.

"Okay, remember that I told you I took over the business after my dad died?" Logan said, and Tessa nodded. "Well, I was in the CIA before that and had to retire from it. I have several contacts in the department still, and Nick is also ex-CIA and ex-military. I wanted to know about the case you told me about, so I did a background on you and the case." He could see that she was livid.

"You what! You did a background on me and looked into the case? You are fucking kidding me! Behind my back? And what gives you the fucking right to do that, you piece of shit?" she said, taking a step closer to him. He could see the rage in her eyes. They looked like the storms that moved in from the ocean.

"Tessa, you were not telling me the whole story, and I just wanted to find out what was going on. I have seen soldiers come back from action with the same things that you are doing with the nightmares and the drinking. I had to check things out—it's my job to keep you safe. I love you, and you mean everything to me now," he said, moving closer to her to look into her eyes. They were still storming, but he also saw something he did not recognize.

Tessa had heard those words before, but she had thought it was a dream. Could it be real? Had he said that to her before? Did he really mean it? She was confused and did not know what to believe now. The only thing she did know was that if Logan and Nick were right about someone following them, they needed to come up with a plan—and now.

"Okay, so who are they, and why are they following you?" she asked, a bit calmer but still alert to her surroundings. She needed more information if she was going to get herself and her father out of there in one piece.

"They are here for you. The head of the cartel that you were working on put a contract out on you to be taken alive because one of the men you killed was his son," Logan said, moving even closer until he was standing in front of her. He placed his hands on her arms, needing to feel her and to make her understand that they were in real danger and needed to get out of there now.

"Okay, so we cannot go back the way we came, and going north is only going to take us farther away from transportation. So, what I think we should do is move northeast for a bit to see if we can move around them before heading due east to where the trucks are. I think that is our best plan because taking a stand here is not a good idea—the cave is not that deep and has no back door."

"How do you know that Daughter?" her father said, looking at her.

"Because, old man, you took me here once years ago. And we walked inside, and you showed me the cave and told me about the area. That is why I knew you would be here," she said, looking at her father. Tessa stepped in front of her father, turned him around, and uncuffed one hand. She turned him back and cuffed his hands in front.

"You might need to use your hands. This will help at least to give you a fighting chance, but do not think for a moment that you will be able to get away. And if you do, I will hunt you down for what you did to Mom.

You need to pay for it. I have taken years of abuse from you. This has to stop—and stop now. So, if you want to get out of here in one piece, stay close to me or one of these guys, because the assholes out there do not give a flying fuck about you and will kill you. Understand?" she said, looking straight at him. He nodded and looked around. Tessa looked through his camp, picked up things she thought might be helpful, packed them in a backpack, and picked it up. She holstered her handgun, checked her rifle, looked around, and pointed to the north for everyone to move out. Logan moved behind Tessa and in front of her father. Nick took up the rear. Logan could tell that she knew which way to go just by the way she moved.

"Okay, I really should not need to tell you all to be quiet. Sound does travel a long way here, so be careful where you are stepping, and no talking. Hand signals only. We might need to spread out more, but I think as long as we are quiet, stay north for a few miles, and turn east, we might be able to move around them. If your weapons have silencers, I would put them on just in case we run into some of them." She showed her rifle with a silencer on it. "Oh, as I am thinking about it, you guys should take a moment to grab some dirt and moss and rub it all over you. Dad, that is how I really found you—by smell. Remember, we might be upwind from them, and they might be able to smell you." She then watched all three men bend down, grab some dirt and moss, and rub it all over before they moved on.

The pace she set was fast, and every once in a while, she would stop, crouch down, and listen. She would smell the air, look around, raise her hand, and signal for them to continue forward. Logan was impressed with her and the way she handled herself out there, but he still was a bit uneasy, not knowing where the group of men were that was following them. Logan was so into his thoughts that he almost ran over Tessa. She was crouched down, listening with her head turned to the right. She raised her hand and signaled for them to get down all the way. Then she put her finger to her mouth and signaled as if to say, "Be quiet, and wait here." She moved silently through the woods and soon was out of sight.

Logan was not happy that he could not see her and did not know where she was. Logan then heard a pop. He motioned for Nick to move closer to her father and stay there as he moved off in the direction Tessa had gone. As he started to go around a tree, a hand came out and pulled him back. A knife was to his throat.

"I told you to stay," said a voice that he knew, and he turned around to see Tessa standing there. The knife had blood on it. He looked her over, and when his eyes reached hers, she saw the question of where the blood had come from.

"We had someone a bit too close, and I was able to get a shot at him. The other guy—well, what can I say? I had to use my knife," she said, bending down and using some moss to clean the blade before moving back toward the others.

"We need to move. They are spread out, and I am afraid we might come up on some of them. Not sure how many of them there are, but now there are two less," she told them before moving northwest, away from the group of strangers she could see and hear. She kept moving at a swift pace, stopping periodically to listen and look around. A few times, she waved the men ahead of her. She would climb a small hill to see if she could see anyone following them and then move quickly back to the men and adjust which way they were moving to keep them away from the group of men she saw behind them.

"We need to hurry; they are getting closer. Or find someplace we can hide," she said to Logan, close to his ear. All he did was nod. She walked up to her father, placed her lips close to his ear, and whispered,

"Do you know of any place where we might go to hide? The group of men behind us is getting closer; not sure we can outrun them now." She looked into his face, hoping he knew of a place. When he nodded, she asked where. He nodded toward the west, so they moved that way.

They soon found a large cave with the entrance under a waterfall. They could hide there, as long as they did not leave any tracks. Tessa told the group to walk in the water to help hide their tracks and walk up the creek before moving under the falls and back into the small cave. The cave gave them a place to hide in that was safe, should there be a firefight.

Tessa removed her backpack and placed it on the floor of the cave. She reached in to grab more ammo and stuffed it into the different pockets of her pants. Checking her handgun and making sure it was good to go, she told her father to stay there and not move. Logan and Nick checked their weapons too and talked quietly between them to set up a plan. Nick was to stay back, and Logan and Tessa stood closer to the mouth of the cave.

She was hoping the waterfall would help to hide them and give them a chance to move away. She needed to get a look at how many there were.

Tessa took a drink of water from her canteen and passed it to Logan to drink. She bent down on the back of her heels and looked out. She put a finger to her lips to show to be quiet and pointed out past the creek.

They had company. Logan saw them. About ten or so men were slowly moving up the creek. They stopped to check the ground, and then they continued to move. Logan lowered to one knee and raised his weapon. He saw that Tessa had readied her weapon as well. The group of men moved closer to the waterfall, and Tessa moved back. Logan followed her lead, and they both moved back and around the corner, hoping no one would come in and look around. Nick came out of the shadows from the back of the small cave.

"I think that we might be able to get out. There is an opening in the back. It is small, but with some digging, I might make it bigger," Nick said, keeping his voice low.

"Not sure if we should—they might hear it, and then we will be trapped. Do you think you can do it quietly?" she said, keeping her voice low too. Nick nodded and moved back to the end of the cave to start digging the hole larger so that they could climb out and away from their pursuers. Tessa and Logan kept an eye on the front of the cave. They could hear a bit of noise from the back of the cave, but she hoped that with the waterfall, the group of men out front would not hear it. The group of men did not move on; they seemed to be waiting for something. They were making themselves comfortable beside the pool that the waterfall fell into. Tessa did not think they knew the cave was there, or else they might have tried to come in and look around. Nick came up quietly from the back of the cave.

"I think the opening is large enough for us to climb through. I fit through it, so I think the rest of you will be able to move through it without any trouble," he said, looking at Logan and then Tessa. Nick took her father to the back of the cave to get him through the opening. Logan moved close to Tessa and whispered into her ear.

"Go. I will be right behind you," he said. Tessa nodded and moved quietly to the back of the cave and up to the opening. She saw that Nick had been able to climb out, so she should have no problem, as she was smaller. Logan was right behind her; he had to move his shoulders sideways to be able to climb out of the opening. He was the bigger of all of them.

Tessa moved to the front to continue west until she thought it was safe to head north, away from the group that was following them. They walked for about an hour before she turned the group north, checking the compass on her knife hilt to make sure she was heading the way she wanted. The sun was starting to set, and they were nowhere close to the spot where she was hoping to be before dark. Tessa found a spot back in the trees with a hill behind them. It was someplace to make camp for the night.

"No fire—we cannot take the chance that they will see it and spot us. I would suggest that we each take a turn at watch and let the others get some sleep. All but you," Tessa said, pointing at her father. Logan walked up to her.

"I will take the first watch; you need to rest. Then Nick can take the next one in about four hours. That will be about the time we can move, so you will not need to worry about pulling watch," Logan said before placing a kiss on her lips. He pulled her close before letting go and moving toward the trees that would keep them hidden. It was a good place to watch and still be able to keep an eye on the group.

Tessa made sure her father was unable to getaway. She cuffed his left hand to his left. It might have been a bit uncomfortable, but he was not going anywhere. She then found a spot with as few rocks as possible and lay down, taking her knife and handgun out so that they were both close by and ready if she needed them. It did not take long for her to fall asleep. She slept lightly, keeping an ear open for anything. She did not dream and did not have the nightmares she had become used to over the last few months. Nick also slept lightly. His military training had taught him to keep one ear open for danger. Logan kept an eye on Tessa, hoping she would not have a nightmare, which would put them all in danger. But as the hours crawled by, she slept quietly, moving little. Her breathing was slow and deep, letting him know she was sleeping and not just resting.

Four hours later, Logan woke up Nick to take over the watch. Since they had worked together, few words were needed between them. Logan lay down next to Tessa; pulled her into him, letting her head rest on his shoulder; and drifted into a light sleep.

Logan felt a hand on his arm, and he was awake. He looked to see Nick standing over him with his finger to his lips to let him know to be quiet.

"I think we have company. I see some movement downhill by the creek," Nick told Logan in a whisper. Logan looked over to see that Tessa's eyes were open; she was listening to what Nick told him. She moved away from Logan and stood up to move over to the trees to get a look at what Nick was talking about. She moved quietly over to the stand of trees and looked down to the creek, where she spotted a group of elk drinking from the creek. She saw one of the elk lift its head to look around and listen. It lowered its head and continued to drink. Tessa took a breath and moved back quietly and quickly to let them know that all was okay.

"It is only a herd of elk, and if there were anyone around, they would not be drinking from the creek, so we are okay for now," she said, taking a look at the sky. She moved her wrist to show her watch and saw that it was about five o'clock in the morning; the sky was getting lighter. She moved to pick up her stuff and returned her knife and handgun back to her hip.

"I think we should be going. It will be light here soon, and I would like to get as much ground between them and us as we can before we reach the truck," she said.

"How do you know where the trucks are? And if they are still there, what if they are being watched? Just how in the hell do you know this?" Nick said, standing there with his hands on his hips, looking at her as if she had just grown a second head.

"I know right where we are and where the trucks are, and if they are being watched, then we will deal with it at that time," she said to him before walking over to uncuff her father and get him to his feet to move out.

As the group followed her, Logan was a bit concerned as to how she was able to know just where they were and the location of the trucks. Logan walked closer to her, wanting to have a few words with her.

"Can I ask a question?" he said, keeping his voice low. Tessa looked over her shoulder and nodded, so he said, "How is it you know just where we are now?"

Tessa took a quick look behind her and reached into her pocket to pull out a small electronic pad displaying an image of the area. Logan looked at it and smiled. She was getting satellite information on the area they were in. Plus, the map showed red spots on it. He looked up with a question on his face.

"Some of the larger ones are wildlife, and these" she pointed to a few large dot "I think are the ones that have been following us. They are moving west, away from us," she said, putting the pad back in her jacket pocket. Logan just smiled and shook his head before he grabbed her and kissed her. Tessa quickly recovered from the toe-curling kiss that Logan gave her. They continued to walk north with as much speed as the woods would let them. They stopped to rest, and she filled her canteen from the stream.

"Is the water safe here?" Nick asked.

Tessa looked up at him and rolled her eyes. "Yes, it is moving about ten miles an hour over the rocks there, and that is why I know that it is safe. Besides, I grew up in these woods. I have been drinking from these streams all my life. Just how in the hell were you able to keep safe through all the training you military guys had?" She continued to fill the canteen before she stood and walked toward her father to give him a drink. She heard her father laugh quietly before taking the canteen from her.

"So, what type of training did you go through to know this?" Nick asked. Tessa looked at her father before she turned around to answer the question.

"Some of it was from him," she said, pointing at her father as her father smiled, "and some of it was from the deputy US marshal training. I took extra courses to cover different kinds of terrains. Most of it was military training that I took on my own and paid for on my own." She looked directly at Nick. She wanted him to understand that she knew what she was doing and had been trained to be the best.

"Besides, I grew up in these woods and understand them. Also, I have this to help us get to where we need to go safely," she said, holding out the pad she had shown Logan. Nick took one look, and a smile came over his face. Logan smiled and laughed.

"You see, I only need this to keep an eye on the bad guys. So, we are okay, as they are heading in the wrong direction and away from us. And look here." She pointed to the pad to show a spot to the northeast. There were no red spots in that area.

"That is where the trucks are, and it looks like no one is watching them. So, we might be able to get out of here before they turn back," she said, placing the pad back in her pocket and moving to help her father up to continue on their way.

CHAPTER 9

AFTER SEVERAL HOURS, THEY REACHED THE trucks. After taking a look around to make sure there was no one there, she walked up to her truck, and that was when she spotted the tires. All of them were flat.

"Fuck, I did not think they would do this. So, I guess we need a plan B. Can you guys hot-wire a car? Because I am sure they did not leave the keys in it," she said, moving toward a black SUV to see if it was locked. It was not, but there were no keys in it.

"I think I can handle it, as this is just one of my many talents," Nick said, laughing. He slipped into the seat to lean in and under the dash, grab a few wires, and strip some to twist together. The motor turned over. Tessa opened the door, moved her father into the backseat, and climbed in next to him. Logan rode shotgun, and Nick closed his door, put the SUV in gear, and drove down the road. Tessa had made sure none of the trucks or SUVs could be driven out of there. She'd flattened all the tires and taken parts off the motors so that the engines would not start. Furthermore, she knew they would need a satellite phone to get any phone message out of there because there was no signal for cell phones.

"You need to turn around and head back the way you came. It will be faster that way. When you come to the T, take a right, and continue. I will let you know which way to go from there," Tessa said.

"So why not use the navigator here?" Nick asked, pointing to the OnStar GPS system.

"Because these roads are not part of the maps they have. These are logging roads, and the navigator would be lost. Besides, you have me, and I know just which way would be the best," she said, leaning forward to take her pack off and reaching into it to get out some trail mix to give to her father to eat. She asked the guys if they wanted some, and then she ate some and put the rest away. Tessa checked the pad and saw a red spot following them. She had Nick drive off the road and up into the tree line on an old logging road that had not been used in years. She had him continue up and around a bend so that they were hidden from the road. Tessa opened the door and stepped out. Logan opened his door and stepped out also.

"Stay here. I am going to take a look and see. I will be back, and here—take this just in case." She handed Logan a walkie-talkie. "I will let you know if you need to go on. Dad knows the way out of here, and he can take you."

"No, I am going with you. Besides, you need backup, and Nick can get your father out of here," Logan said, giving a clear message that he would not take no for an answer.

"No, you will only slow me down should I need to move fast. I know these woods. You do not, and Nick needs you—he cannot drive and shoot if needed. So no, you are not going with me," she said, taking a step toward him, looking him straight in the eyes, and giving him her best "Do not fuck with me" look.

"Nice try, sweetheart, but I am still going. And Nick is able to drive and shoot, so I am coming," Logan said, and then he kissed her senseless before shutting the door, stepping away from the SUV, and handing Nick the walkie-talkie.

"I will let you know what is going on—if you need to leave or if we will be back. So, wait for my signal, Nick," Logan said, moving away from the SUV to follow Tessa.

She moved up the hill and away from the SUV to get a look at their surroundings. Logan watched as she moved through the woods with grace and speed, making little noise. Each time he would step wrong and make noise, she would turn around and almost growl at him, giving him a hard look. Just as she was able to step out of the tree line to get a better look, she dropped down to one knee quickly and signaled to Logan to do the same. She could see the road, and their pursuers could also have a clear line of sight to them. Tessa pulled out her rifle and used the scope to see. There were four guys in the truck: two inside and two outside in the bed standing up against the bed of the truck. Each had a gun, and it was not hunting season there yet, so they were out of place. She turned to Logan and, with a knowing look, told him they were being followed.

He took her face in his hands, kissed her, and pulled her close. Logan slowly pulled back to look into her eyes. He wanted to see what she was thinking about, and what he saw brought a smile to his face. There in her face, he saw passion, desire, and longing—all the things he was feeling and hoping to see. Logan hoped that someday he could make her see that she could not live without him either.

Tessa was feeling things she had never felt before, things she had dreamed of years ago but had given up when all the men in her life had beaten her down. How could she let him in and trust him with her heart? She could see all of the things in his eyes she was feeling, but the one thing she needed to see in his eyes was love. Could he love her and continue to feel all of this and not break her heart later, as the rest had done?

"You should have told me sooner. I could have been better prepared, and I needed to know what was coming my way. Keeping this from me shows you have no trust in me and don't believe that I can and will protect myself and my family, whom they might be going after. How could you do this?" she said. He could see the hurt in her eyes and hated that he had put it there. Logan did not know how to answer her question; he knew only that he felt the need to protect her and keep her safe.

"Nick? Over," Logan said into the walkie-talkie.

"Nick here. Over," he replied.

"We have eyes on a truck, and they are coming your way. Stay there. These are not the good guys, from the looks of them. Over," Logan said.

"Copy that. Over," said Nick.

Tessa pulled out the pad and saw two other trucks on the same road. She was not sure if they were part of the same group, but she did not want to take a chance. Tessa looked around and checked out the road up ahead of the truck, and she found a spot that would be great to get the truck off the road: a steep downhill slope on the left-hand side. If she could just shoot the driver and have the truck go off the road, they might be able to take out their followers.

Tessa explained what she wanted to do, and Logan nodded, placed one of the rifles from her father up against his shoulder, and waited. Tessa raised her rifle and took aim at the driver. Just before she pulled the trigger, she told Logan to take out as many as he could. She then pulled the trigger and watched as the two men in the back of the truck jerked backward and fell, and the truck drove off the road to the left, going down the steep mountainside.

Tessa looked back at the pad to see how close the other truck was and to see if the vehicle was a threat or just someone driving around the mountain for fun. Tessa signaled for Logan to follow her; she wanted to get back watching for the truck coming. They moved through the woods, keeping close to the trees, stopping from time to time to listen and look around.

Tessa was just moving around a tree, when a hand came out of nowhere, grabbed her, and pulled her forward. Logan saw that someone was next to Tessa, but before he could do anything, someone knocked him on the back of his head, and he dropped to the ground as blood flowed from the back of his head.

Tessa pulled out of the hands that had grabbed her and dropped down to the ground. She rolled to one of her shoulders, trying to get to her feet to pull her gun out. She was able to get a shot off and hit one of the men before another one grabbed her, pulled his fist back, and hit her on the side of her head. Tessa was knocked back, and her vision was foggy; she could taste the metallic flavor of blood in her mouth. Before she could get her senses about her, she was pulled up, and her hands were tied behind her back. Her guns and backpack were taken from her.

"You have caused a lot of problems, and my employer wants you alive and in one piece, but from the look of you, I would not mind a part of you myself," said the man before he kissed her hard and tried to put his tongue in her mouth. Tessa spit in his face, and he said.

"No? Well, suit yourself. You might change your mind before we get you back to my employer."

"Over my fucking dead body, asshole," Tessa said to the man as he wiped his face, and he snarled at her.

"Oh, it will be my pleasure, princess, to see that you get what is coming to you before my employer gets what he wants. I will make sure," the man said as he grabbed her and pulled her beside him and down to the road.

"Hey, what do you want to do with this one? He is still breathing, boss," one of the guys said.

"Kill him, but be quiet about it," the man said to the guy standing over Logan.

"No. Leave him alone; he does not know anything," Tessa said, scared they would kill Logan. She found that for some reason, she was more scared than she had ever been.

"Help! Stop! Help me! Please, someone, help me!" Tessa screamed at the top of her voice, hoping that the sound would carry, and that Nick might hear it and do something to help Logan.

"Shut up, bitch," the man said before hitting her again. This time, the blow knocked her out.

Nick was sitting there waiting when he heard what sounded like a few pops and something crashing. Nick stepped out of the truck and looked toward the sounds.

"Let me go! They might need help. I might be an asshole, but I do not want my daughter to die. Let me go!" her father yelled at Nick. Nick turned around, grabbed the cuffs, and unlocked them. Then Nick grabbed his gun and turned to her dad.

"Okay, let's go see what is going on. Something is not right about this—I have a feeling. Stay close to me, and here—just in case there is trouble," Nick said, handing a handgun to him with a nod. Nick and her dad walked quietly and quickly toward where Nick had heard the noise, and they came upon a group of men. One had Tessa, and Logan was on the ground. Nick did not know if Logan was dead or just out cold. He watched as the guy holding Tessa kissed her, and when she spit on him, a small smile formed on Nick's face. He looked beside him at her dad, and the look on his face was murderous.

As a man stepped toward Logan and raised his gun to Logan's head, a pop sounded, and the man fell. The rest of the group dropped down and took cover, not knowing which way the shot had come from. The man who had Tessa moved back, taking her with him. Looking around but not seeing anyone, he put a gun to her head and said, "Whoever the fuck you are, stop now, or I will kill her." When no more shots were heard, the man continued to move backward, taking Tessa with him.

"Cover my back so I can get her out of here," the man said, and he picked Tessa up and placed her on his shoulder before leaving.

Nick moved to the left, and her dad moved to the right; each one started to take out the remaining men in the group. They both kept moving, not giving the group a chance to locate them. When all in the group were dead or running, Nick stepped out of the trees, ran to Logan, and knelt down. Logan was still alive but out cold, with blood coming from the back of his head.

Logan felt as if a two-ton truck had hit him as he started to wake up. He felt as if his head were going to split wide open. He'd never had it hurt this bad, not even during the many hangovers he'd had when he was younger.

"It's about time you woke up, dude. We do not have all the time in the world to wait on your ass," Nick said, crouched next to him. Logan sat up, and a wave of nausea hit him. He became dizzy, as Logan stood up Nick reached out and grabbed him just before Logan fell. Logan bent over and threw up until there was nothing left in his stomach.

"How long have I been out?" Logan said, wiping his mouth and standing up. He felt a bit better but still had one hell of a headache. He looked at Nick and then at Tessa's father. Then he looked around more but found it hard to see, as it was dark. With no fire and only the light in Nick's hand. "How long, Nick?"

Nick looked at him and then took a breath. "Four hours," Nick said.

"How is Tessa? You saved her, right?" Logan looked around, hoping to see her sitting nearby or walking toward him. When Nick did not answer, Logan looked at him again.

"Where is she, Nick? You did not let them take her, did you? Do you have any idea what they are going to do to her?" he said, grabbing Nick by the front of his shirt and pushing him backward. "How could you let them take her, Nick? Why?"

"We tried to save her, but the man who had her knocked her out, and the rest kept us busy so that he could get away. There was nothing I or Nick could do," her father said, looking at Logan.

Logan felt as if his world had just cracked apart. It was his job to keep her safe, and he'd failed. Now dangerous men had her, and they would kill her if he did not save her.

"Come on. They are not looking for us, just her, so we need to go—now. I need to locate her and try to rescue her before they kill her. I just hope they have not left the country yet. If so, we are screwed," Logan said. Looking around, he spotted her backpack and saw the pad she had been using to track their followers. He picked it up and wiped his hand over it, and the screen glowed and showed the area, with some spots that he figured were wildlife.

"Let's go. Which way is the SUV? We need to get out of here now," Logan said, grabbing her backpack and placing it over his shoulder. He found comfort in the fact that it smelled like her. He breathed in deeply and closed his eyes, remembering the time they'd spent in his house and the time he had her in his arms as she slept in his bed. Logan took a step and stopped when he did not feel them following him.

"What is the problem? We need to go now. Why are you not moving?"

"Wrong way, dude. This way—I moved the truck. It is just down the hill, on the road," Nick said, and he moved downhill toward the road. Logan turned and followed. He was still unsteady and knew he should have someone look at his head, but there was no time. Logan could feel the slow burn of outrage, and he dug deep to find his calm place. To get her back, he needed to be able to think clearly and keep his emotions under control. He had already failed to keep her safe. He had been trained for this, so he pushed deep to connect with his training and years of experience to plan a way to rescue her and bring her home to him.

CHAPTER 10

TESSA WOKE UP SLOWLY, AND THE first thing she felt was the pain in her head and on her mouth. Her hands were still tied behind her, and she sat up to look around. She heard voices speaking in Spanish. They were talking about what they were going to do when they delivered her to Joaquin, and they discussed the rewards they would get for bringing her to him. She was glad they had not tied her feet, as she might have a chance to getaway. As she turned to look around more, a man turned toward her.

"You are awake. Good. We are almost there, and that is when the fun will begin. I talked to my employer and asked him if I might have some time with you before he talks to you," the man said, looking at her with lust in his eyes.

"You do know that I will kill you if you so much as lay a hand on me, right, asshole?" she said slowly and quietly, wanting only him to hear her words.

"Oh, I do not think so, princess. We are going to have so much fun. You will enjoy yourself, and do not think of killing me, sweetheart," he said, rubbing his thumb down her cheek. Tessa did not move; she only looked at him, thinking of different ways to kill him and trying to decide which one she would enjoy most when the time came.

She thought of Logan and wondered what had happened to him. *Is he okay? Did they kill him? And what about Nick and Dad? What happened to them? Was it Nick and my father who shot at the group? Did they die?*

When the man turned and looked out the front window of the SUV they were riding in, she knew that if she did not carefully use the training and experience she had, she would never get out of there by herself. She turned her mind inward to think of the many different ways to approach this situation and of which one would work. Some she dismissed as unworkable, and others had only a small chance.

As she was thinking through a plan, the SUV slowed and turned into a driveway with a large gate. She could not see much, as she was on the floor of the backseat. She sensed the SUV slowing down, and then it came to a stop. The door opened, and the man who had grabbed her in the woods reached in, grabbed her, and pulled her out of the SUV.

Tessa kicked him in his genitals, stood up, and ran. She dropped to her shoulder to roll her feet under her hands and bring her hands in front of her. As she stood up, the first guy grabbed her. She turned quickly, swung her fist at him, and knocked him down. Then she took off running toward the gate. Seeing its closing, she was not sure if she would be able to make it, when someone tackled her and threw her to the ground. She rolled and jumped to her feet, seeing someone coming. She swung her foot at his head and knocked him down. She could see that the gate was closed. She looked around and found that it was surrounded by a ten-foot rock wall. She took off running toward the gate, confident she could climb it. Before she was able to take a few steps, someone grabbed her, and she saw a knife come at her. She sidestepped and hit the man in the back. He dropped the knife, and she grabbed it and took several more steps before she was stopped again by someone else.

Tessa used the knife as a weapon. No one had fired a gun at her, because they wanted her alive. She dropped on one leg and did a leg sweep to kick his legs out from under him before she bashed him in the head with the handle of the knife and took off running again.

She could hear them looking for her as she ran into some bushes, trying to find someplace to stop just for a moment to cut the ropes off of her wrists.

"How could you let her go, and why have you not found her yet? The gates are closed and guarded, and so are all the other gates. Where in the hell is she, James? How could one little female get away from you? Find her! Do you hear me, James?" Joaquin said, not happy one bit. "And do not hurt her! Understand?" Joaquin said, looking at James.

"Yes, sir, I understand. She will not get away. We will find her, and I told them not to harm her, sir. I will take care of it. Do not worry," James said, looking at Joaquin, who turned and walked into the mansion.

"Find her—now!" James shouted at the men standing around him. He was still rubbing his balls—where she had kicked him. *She is going to pay for this*, he thought, and he knew just what he was going to do. With that thought, he smiled before turning to walk into the mansion and to the computer room, where all the security cameras were recording. He might find her that way if he was lucky.

Tessa cut off the ropes. Now that her hands were free, she might be able to get out of there. She listened and heard someone walking by, so she stayed behind the large bush she was hiding behind until the person walked by. She did not hear anyone else, so she slowly came out, looking both ways and keeping low. It was getting dark, and that helped. She continued moving from bush to bush or whatever would hide her. She looked around, trying to find some way out of this place. She had made it to the garage, which was more like a house with ten large doors. She walked behind it and found that she could use a barrel to get up onto the roof. From there, she could use a tree branch over the garage to get onto the rock wall.

Tessa was on the barrel and pulling herself up to the roof when someone stepped around the side of the garage and saw her.

"Found her!" yelled the person running around the side of the garage. Tessa pulled herself up, jumped to the limb, hooked her arm over it, and pulled her leg up and over so that she was sitting on the limb. Then she crawled over to the tree and then the rock wall. One of the guards quickly climbed up onto the roof. Tessa made it to the rock wall, and she then heard a voice behind her.

"Stop, or I will shoot you, bitch," said James, the one she had kicked in the balls. He had a gun pointed at her.

"Nice try, asshole, but the boss wants me alive and in one piece. I heard him myself, so fuck you," she said just before she jumped down on the other side of the rock wall. As she landed, hands grabbed her and pushed her to the ground. She saw James walking toward her with a twisted smile on his face.

Once again, she found herself tied up; they had taken the knife from her as she was being pulled along behind the man called James, the boss's right hand. She had been so close to getting out, and now she was trapped inside the mansion with lots of guards and no weapon to use. She was untied and told to clean up; then the door shut and locked. Tessa looked around, hoping for anything she could use to protect herself and maybe get out of there. She walked into the bathroom and looked at herself in the mirror. Her eye was swollen, her lip was split, and she had a big black-and-blue mark on the left side of her face. She washed up, there was not much she could do about her clothes, but why worry about that when she did not know if she would still be alive or what was going to happen to her?

She heard the door open, followed by heavy footsteps into the other room. She walked to the door just as someone knocked on it. She opened the door to see James standing by a table with food and drinks on it. She kept her distance from him, not knowing what he was up to, remembering the statement he'd made about having some fun and his wicked smile; she did not think she was going to like what he had in mind.

"Sit and eat; you look like you could use a meal and something to drink. I have wine. Would you like a glass?" James asked.mn

"No," she said with rage in her voice.

"You might as well have something to eat and drink; you will be here a long time. Plenty of time for me to get to know you—and you me, if you know what I mean, sweetheart," James said, taking a step closer. Tessa stepped back, keeping several steps away from him and making sure he could not trap her in a corner.

"You might as well make yourself at home because I will not be giving you up for a long time. Boss said I could take all the time I want with you, and when I am done, he gets you. It can be pleasurable, or I can make it painful—it is your choice, sweetheart," James said as he poured a glass of wine for himself and sat down in a chair.

"First of all, I am not your sweetheart, asshole. I will be your nightmare if you come at me. I have ways to make you think twice before touching me, dumbass, and that is not a threat; it is a promise," she said, making sure to keep him in her sight as she slowly made her way toward the door, hoping it was not locked. As she was getting closer to the door and away from him, she saw him start to eat, not even looking at her.

She reached the door and turned the knob. The door was unlocked. She opened the door and took a step into the hall, only to find two guards standing there, blocking her way. She kicked one and then flipped over to stand behind the other one. She kicked him in the back, making him fall into the other guard, and she took off running, only to find two more guards at the end of the hall.

Tessa locked her knees and took a stand, waiting for them to come at her and keeping an eye on the ones behind her. Something was not right. James stood in the doorway, watching and sipping his wine, waiting to see what she would do. Tessa looked at James and then turned to see one of the guards with a Taser in his hand, pointed at her. She looked back at James to see him smiling at her and leaning against the doorjamb.

"So, babe, are you ready to play nice? Because you might have been able to get through these two jerks, but I really do not think you will be able to get away from the Taser." James waved his hand toward the room, signaling for her to move into it. Tessa's fury was off the charts; she was so mad that she was shaking. She walked by James and heard him snicker at her, and she walked into the bathroom, slammed the door, and locked it. Tessa leaned against the vanity and looked at her face in the mirror; she was tired and in pain and needed to sleep. If need be, she would stay there and try to sleep in the tub. There were big towels she could use. She sat down against the vanity and closed her eyes, wanting to fall asleep and find this was a bad dream when she woke up.

CHAPTER 11

LOGAN AND NICK REACHED THE TOWN and were not sure what to do with her dad now that they were there. Logan turned to him and then looked at Nick.

"So, what are we to do with you? I have not a clue what she was going to do, and I really do not have time to deal with you or your shit. I need to find Tessa, and I need every moment now," Logan said to her father.

"I know what to do, and I will take care of it. Just see if you can find her. I have been so wrong about everything and about her, so please find her and bring her home safe and sound. Please," her father said to Logan, and he reached out his hand to shake Logan's hand and then Nick's before turning and walking away.

Logan stood there for a moment and just watched as he walked away. Nick was just as lost as to what to do or how to do it. Logan reached for his phone and put in a call to the one man he knew who would help him and who had the power to make it happen. After Logan made the call, he and Nick drove to the airport to catch a flight to Washington, DC, and to the one man who would help find her.

The trip took several hours. Logan purchased a laptop, logged on using the Wi-Fi on the plane, and started to research everything he could using the database he was given access to, trying to find out where Joaquin might be. He hoped he was not too late. Nick slept most of the way to Washington, DC, and when they had landed, both of them picked up clothes to change into before going to see the director of the CIA, who was a close friend to them both.

Logan would never have asked for a favor like this, but he needed the resources that the CIA had and the information on the drug lord to help him get Tessa back. Logan had a single mission, and its name was Tessa. He needed to get her back alive and safe, and he would do anything to make it happen; he would even kill the drug lord and every one of his fucked-up men.

Logan walked into the building where he'd worked for several years before he retired to take over the family business. Most of the guards still knew him by name, and they called out and reached out to shake his hand as well as Nick's. Both men had worked together for years, so when Logan had asked Nick to work for him, Nick had been happy to. Besides, the pay was better, and no one was shooting at him—until now.

They had a meeting behind closed doors to see what information Logan could get and what plans might be in the works. They were at the meeting for six hours, going over every picture and everything else they had on the drug lord and those who worked for him. When a picture of James came up, Logan jumped up.

"Who is this?" he asked.

"He is Joaquin's second-in-command. His name is James. We really do not have much on him besides a few pictures and a name. Why?" the director asked.

"Because that is the asshole who grabbed Tessa. I saw him just before someone hit me from behind."

"Yes, I saw him, and he was the one who hit Tessa, knocked her out, and carried her out of the woods before all hell blew up around us," Nick said.

"We have to find her—and soon. All I know is that Joaquin wants to kill her, and I mean he wants to pull the trigger himself because she killed his son," Logan said, shaking with rage.

He walked over to the window to look out, and his thoughts turned to Tessa and the way she looked when standing on his deck and looking out to sea or sleeping. Logan breathed in deeply and lowered his head to his chest with his arms across his chest. He felt the time was running out and worried they were not going to find her in time. He could hear her laughing in his head. He loved her sass, the way she would stand up to him, how good it was when he kissed her, and the way she fit next to him in every way. The door opened, and in walked a man with folders.

"I think we have them. Here are some pictures taken just about eight hours ago in LA. We have been able to ID James and Joaquin, but there is a woman with them we do not know, and it might be the woman you are looking for," said the man, handing the pictures to Logan. There in black and white was Tessa. She looked okay besides the bruises covering her face.

"Do you know where Joaquin is now?" Logan asked the man.

"Yes, this is the address. We have done a background check, and it all checks out. The mansion is rented under Joaquin's name, and we have the plans to it here," the man said, handing Logan a blueprint of the mansion to study. Logan looked at the plans to find the best way to get her out of there, but first, they needed to know where she was being kept.

"Do you have any information on her location inside the mansion that could help us plan this?" Logan asked. The man shook his head. They did not have anything further.

Logan and Nick called the airport to get flights to LA as quickly as possible. They now knew where she was, and Logan was one step closer to getting her home to him, where she belonged.

*   *   *

Tessa woke up in a bed with the covers over her and the sun shining in through the window. She sat up, trying to remember how she had gotten there. The last thing she remembered was sitting in the bathroom on the floor and feeling tired, and now there she was, in a bed, covered up, still wearing the same clothes she'd worn last night. She threw the covers back and turned to put her feet on the floor when she heard a voice.

"Now, why would you want to get up, when I want you right there in bed with me for as long as I want? And right now, I want it," said James, who was sitting in a chair, wearing cotton pants that hung low on his hips. He did not have a shirt on. Tessa saw what looked like breakfast sitting on the table, and she saw that his clothes from the night before were on the floor. She turned and looked over to see that the side of the bed looked as if someone had been there last night. She stood and walked into the bathroom to find that the lock had been removed. She turned to James with disgust and then continued to walk into the bathroom and closed the door. She was washing her face when the door opened, and James walked in, holding some clothes.

"Thought you might like to shower and change," he said. Tessa looked at the clothes without saying anything to him. James placed the pile of clothes on the vanity, walked back out of the room, and closed the door.

Tessa looked at the clothes on the vanity and then saw how dirty her own clothes were. A shower did sound great, so she took off her clothes, started the shower, and stepped under the water. All she felt was delight as she washed her hair and body. After stepping out, wrapping a towel around her hair, and drying off with another towel, she grabbed the clothes James had given her and quickly dressed.

She brushed out her hair and braided it so that it lay down the middle of her back, and then she opened the door and walked out, finding James talking to one of the guards. He looked up, smiled at her, and dismissed the guard.

"So now are you hungry? There is plenty to eat, and you did not eat last night. In fact, I waited for an hour while you were in the bathroom. When you did not come out, I had the lock taken off, and you looked very uncomfortable sitting on the floor, so I carried you to bed. I enjoyed having you wrapped around me most of the night after I crawled into bed later. I love having you next to me—so soft and warm," James said, stepping close and brushing his thumb down her face.

Tessa did not move or blink. James moved to the table to pull out a chair for her. She did not move, and a look of hatred shined in her eyes. If looks could have killed, James would have been ash on the floor. Tessa lifted her chin and walked to the window to look out. She was not going to let him get what he wanted; she was not going to give in, no matter what. James walked up behind her; she could feel the heat from him. She crossed her arms over her chest. James placed his hands on her shoulders, rubbing his thumbs gently into her shoulder muscles.

"I know you must be hungry. You did not eat last night, and I need you to eat to keep up your strength. You will need it, love." He lowered his head to kiss her neck, but just before he landed on her neck, she sidestepped him and moved away toward the table to fill a plate of food. She sat down to eat, keeping one eye on James. He slowly walked back to the table and sat down in the chair across from her. Tessa was hungry, but she was not going to let him know that. He was right; she needed to eat to keep her strength up to be able to fight her way out when she was given the opportunity.

"Let me make this very clear for you: I am the only reason you will continue breathing. This is my suite for as long as I want you. This is where you will be, and when I no longer want you, then the boss man will get you. It's the deal I have with him, so it would be better to keep me happy. Understand, sweetheart?" James said with a wicked smile.

Tessa stopped eating. She was having trouble thinking and was shaking because she was so angry. Tessa grabbed a handful of food and threw it at him. She stood so fast that the chair she was sitting in fell over behind her.

"If those are my only choices, then just hand me over to him, because I will never let you touch me!" Tessa screamed with all the fury and hatred she had inside. James wiped the food off his face. He was furious. He stood, walked around the table, and stood toe to toe with her, looking down into her eyes.

James grabbed her and pulled her close to him before crushing his lips onto hers. He ran his tongue along her lips, wanting her to open her mouth for him. Tessa pushed him back and slapped him across his face, leaving a red handprint on it. She took a step back.

"I said never! Do not touch me!"

"We will see, sweetheart. I will have you one way or the other, but mark my words: I will have you," James said before walking out of the room and shutting the door.

She heard it lock. She took a deep breath, trying to calm down. In her rage, she knocked over the table, sending the food flying all around. She kicked over chairs, knocked over lamps, and threw books before ending up in front of the large picture window.

She fought to never have any man control her. She made dam sure that she was skilled to protect herself. Now look at her, she is here and at the mercy of this man. She could feel the fingers of fear moving up and down her back.

She put her hands on the window and leaned her head on it. No matter what she did, she could not stop the tears from flowing down her face.

Tessa raised her head. From far away, a man with a camera took a picture of her to add to the many he had been taking.

Tessa stood up and wiped away the tears, knowing they did not help and were a sign of weakness. She was not weak, not by a long shot. She walked into the bedroom to see if there was anything she could use to escape. She saw lots of James's clothes, so she knew this was his suite. After searching for it, she did not find any women's clothes other than the dress she was wearing.

"Sick fucking bastard," Tessa whispered as she moved into the walk-in closet and knocked on the walls, hoping to find a door where they'd hid guns or something to help her get out of there. She would not give up trying, no matter what they did to her.

"What are you looking for, sweetheart?" said a voice dripping with anger. Tessa turned her head to look over her shoulder and saw James leaning on the doorjamb with his arms crossed over his chest. James was six foot four and had black hair that curled just past his ears. His eyes were bright blue, and his face had strong lines, almost as if carved from stone. His chest showed that he worked out, and his arms were well toned, with muscles that only came from hours of working out. He had six-pack abs and a trim waist and hips. His pants hung low on his hips, and his feet were bare.

Tessa moved her eyes left and right, knowing she was trapped in there with little room to move around. James pushed off and took a step toward her. Tessa stepped back and around a table in the middle of the room, keeping it between them; she could still see her handprint on his face as he slowly moved toward her. Tessa continued to walk around the table to keep it between her and James. When Tessa was in front of the door, she quickly walked out into the bedroom, trying to put more distance between them. Tessa knew there was no place she could hide to be safe. She watched as James walked out of the closet.

"I see you have a temper. I hope that you feel better now, my little wildcat," James said, walking up to her. Tessa had her back up against the large picture window in the bedroom, which looked out into the front of the mansion. James placed his hands on her arms and rubbed his thumbs around on her shoulders. He lowered his mouth, and just as his lips touched hers, she moved her head to the side. James kissed and nipped the side of her face and worked down to her neck, kissing and nipping. One hand wrapped around her waist to pull her closer, and his other hand reached around her neck to pull her head around. James grabbed a handful of hair to pull her face up. Then he slipped his lips over hers. Tessa became stiff in his arms. She did not return the kiss; in fact, she did everything she could to break it off. Tessa tried to push him off, but there was no room; he had her locked against him. She could not get any room between them, for her arms were locked between them.

Tessa felt him lift her, walk over to the bed, lay her down, and cover her. She tried to move and stop him from taking her, and just when she'd thought she had lost, she heard someone cough in the room, and she knew it was not James.

CHAPTER 12

THE MAN WITH THE CAMERA CONTINUED to take pictures, zooming in to get shots in the room. He could not help but feel sorry for her when her face was against the window and tears were falling down her face. He did not like to think of what she was going through and what would happen to her if they did not get her out of there soon. The man moved quickly away to show the team which room she was in and how they might get her out.

He hated that he could not help her and that she was trapped in there with so much evil, but he hoped they might be able to get to her before it was too late. He was a bit confused as to why she was with the second-in-command when Joaquin was the one who wanted her dead.

James lifted his head to look over his shoulder at the person who'd made the mistake of coming into his bedroom when he had her just where he wanted her. James rolled over and came to his feet to see a guard standing at the door, looking nervous. Tessa rolled over to get to the other side of the king-size bed and closer to the bathroom. She jumped off the bed, ran to the bathroom, and slammed the door.

"Sorry, but the boss wants to talk to you now," said the guard, turning to leave, hoping to get out of there before being killed by James. For he had a reputation for not thinking twice before killing someone who pissed him off. James watched the guard quickly leave.

"We are not done here, sweetheart. I will be back, and we will continue—make no mistake on that," James said, and he walked out to go see what the boss wanted. Then he would return to get her into his bed. He wanted to know if she was as hot as he thought. James had to adjust his pants before going to see the boss.

Tessa leaned against the door and hoped he would not come in, realizing how close she'd come to getting raped by him. She heard him tell her he would be back and then walk away. Tessa opened the door and looked out to see that the room was empty. She walked out and into the living room. She spotted two people in it, cleaning up the mess she'd made in her rage; one was a woman, and the other was a man. Both looked up at her as she walked in.

Tessa reached down to pick up a broken dish when a hand stopped her, and the woman nodded. As Tessa looked at the man, he too nodded, and she saw him move his eyes up. Tessa looked behind her and spotted the camera with a red light on.

"Just fucking great," she said, and then she reached for a broken chair leg, threw it at the camera hanging from the wall, and broke it off. "Take that, you motherfucker!" she screamed. Tessa walked into the bedroom to see if there was a camera in there too. When she found it, she threw a lamp at it and broke it too. Next, she checked out the bathroom and found one there, and she did the same thing.

"Take that, asshole. No more free looks." She turned to walk out of the bathroom and heard voices from the living room, belonging to the two people who were cleaning up the mess.

"Do you think they will blame us? I did not think she would do that, and from the looks of this room, I think she did this too," said the man, continuing to pick up the broken stuff as the woman started to vacuum the room.

"I really hope not. I mean, it is not our problem, and they saw her do it. I really do hope she does not get into too much trouble over it," the woman said, turning on the vacuum cleaner and working it over the rug and floors. Tessa did not move into the room; she walked over to the window and looked out, trying to think of a way to get out of this mess and back home.

* * *

Hours later, after the photographer had developed the pictures, he handed them over to the team. Two extra men who were ex-CIA and trained for this type of case were now part of the team. The photographer placed the folder with the pictures of the mansion on the table for everyone to look at, and the director of the CIA said.

"Logan, Nick, this is Dean. He is one of the shadow units we used to get the needed information. He's involved in many of the cases we work on, and you both might have used the information Dean was able to get. Dean, this is Logan and Nick; they are working with the team. They both are ex-CIA. They have a great deal of experience with this type of case; plus, Logan has a personal interest in it."

The men shook hands all around, and Logan grabbed the folder and opened it. The first picture was of Tessa in front of the window, crying and bruised. The only thing he felt at that moment was white-hot rage. Logan placed both hands on the table and leaned on it; his body was stiff and shaking with fury. Nick placed a hand on his shoulder and gave it a hard squeeze.

"I understand, bro, but you need to dial it down, or you will be no help to her. I understand that you feel like you failed her but look she is still alive. That's something, right?" Nick watched as Logan slowly took control of the rage burning through him at seeing the pictures, including one of James attacking her. Logan had never in his life wanted to kill someone until now, and he had James in his sight.

"Okay, we now have the place under surveillance, and we have pictures of the player and plans to the place. We can start to make plans to find a way to rescue the deputy US marshal and place Joaquin under arrest for the death of the deputy US marshal's team and the kidnap of Deputy US Marshal Miller, as seen in this picture, plus dozens of other charges at least," the director said, pointing to Tessa's picture. Then they went over ideas and plans to meet these goals with little to no injury to his staff or Logan and Nick.

Logan could see the pain in her eyes in the picture of her at the window, and his heart felt heavy. Nick watched him and could see the tight control that Logan had on his emotions, as well as the pain in his eyes after looking at the pictures and thinking about what they might mean.

* * *

Tessa stood there. She did not know for how long. The light slowly faded, and night came. Her mind was going over and over plans, considering which ones would work and which would not. She had little information to be able to make a good plan; she might need to wing it and see how far she could get without getting caught or killed. She did not feel him until his hands were on her, and she became rigid. Her senses were on high alert.

"I hear that my wildcat was at it again and destroyed more of the things in my room. What? You do not like being watched? I see. If I told you that there are other cameras that cannot be seen and that can also hear every word anyone in these rooms says, what would you do, my wildcat?" He lowered his head to kiss her neck before he turned her around, placed his lips on hers, and pulled her closer. He noticed she did not fight, nor did she react. James pulled back and looked at her. He saw her eyes shining with rage and hatred, and he could see the loathing on her face.

"I told you before I left that we would finish this when I came back, and I fully intend to, with your blessing or not. It would be better if you gave your blessing; you might enjoy it. I have been told that I am a good lover. Besides, you are beautiful and in need of being loved," James said before kissing her again or at least trying to. He was about to pick her up and take her to the bedroom when someone knocked on the door.

"It had better be important, or someone is going to die!" James yelled at the door. A moment later, it opened, and in walked Joaquin dressed in a suit, followed by two soldiers, who closed the door.

"Boss, to what do I owe the pleasure of your visit? As you can see, I am a bit busy. Perhaps this could wait, say, for a least a few hours," James said, not caring that the man who had just walked in cared little for anyone and had killed more than his share of people—if not by his hand, then by ordering others to do it.

"James, I just wanted to let you know that something has come up. I will be leaving town for a few days—something I need to take care of. I am putting you in charge. See that you follow my plans, as we talked about." Joaquin walked over to Tessa. As he stood in front of her, he thought, *this woman is beautiful. What a shame she will be dead soon.*

"It is my pleasure to meet you, at last, my dear. I have seen many pictures of you, and you are more beautiful in person. When I get back, I hope to spend some time with you and talk, if I may," Joaquin said.

"Why would I want to talk to you after what you did to my team and me? You are everything that I stand against and work hard in taking down.

Mark my words: you will go down—if not by my hand, then by someone else's. That is a promise," Tessa said with her shoulders back, and her head held high, looking him in the eye, not showing one bit of fear at knowing that this man was going to kill her.

"James, I think you might need help with this one, and I agree Wildcat is a good name for her. Bye, my dear." With that, Joaquin left with his guards behind him.

"Not a wise thing to piss off the boss, Wildcat," James said, looking at her with his arm around her. He pulled her close and kissed her neck before he lifted her into his arms to carry her into the bedroom, when someone again knocked on the door.

"I am going to kill someone! What?" James screamed. A moment later, the door opened, and a cart was pushed into the room. The staff began placing food on the table that had replaced the one Tessa destroyed. James placed her back on her feet, took her hand to pull her toward the table, and pulled a chair out for her to sit on. When she did not sit, he pushed her down into it and then removed the knife from the table and gave it back to the staff.

"I know how good you are with knives, so I think it would be best that you do not have them for my safety," James said, smiling, as he walked over and sat down in the chair across from her. The staff placed a plate in front of her. On it was a steak, a baked potato, steamed asparagus, and fresh bread. Tessa looked down at the steak and over to James.

"I am to use my bare hands and eat this like an animal now that I have no knife to cut it with?" she said, her voice dripping with ice and sarcasm. James just smiled and leaned over to cut her steak for her. Then he sat back and smiled at her before taking a bite of his own steak. Tessa was hoping he would give his knife to her to use. She was not going to use it on the steak but on him. She slowly finished her dinner, not knowing what James was going to do and not wanting to find out. James picked up the phone, made a call to have the dinner removed, and then helped her out of the chair. As she stood, he placed one hand on her neck and the other around her waist and pulled her close before placing a kiss on her lips. The kiss was soft and slow. She did not know why she was letting him kiss her. Her arms were heavy, and she was tired. She felt him pick her up and carry her to the bedroom, and that was the last thing she remembered.

*   *   *

Logan was working on the rage that filled his body and was not doing well when Nick told him to stop and get some rest. He needed to be at his best if they were to get her back. Logan knew Nick was right and tried to sleep. They still had a lot of things to work out, and this would be the time to rest. However, each time Logan closed his eyes, all he saw was the picture of her standing at the window with a look of pain on her face and tears falling down. Logan was eventually able to get a few hours of rest, though not as much as he needed. *I need to get her back* was all that was in his thoughts, and even in his dreams, she was in great danger and was yelling for help. He could not get to her no matter how hard he tried.

Logan was running after her as James took her, and he could hear her screaming for Logan to help her as she disappeared into a bank of fog. Her screams woke him. Logan sat straight up with a knife in his hand; his heart slammed against his chest as if he had ran for miles. His breathing was fast. He looked first left and then right and saw Nick walking toward him with a look of concern on his face.

"Are you okay, bro? You look like you are going to kill someone, dude," Nick said, making sure Logan was awake and not still dreaming.

"I'm fine, and yes, I will kill that motherfucker when I get my hands on him—that is a sure fucking bet you can make money on, bro," Logan said, turning to place his feet on the floor before putting on his boots and standing up.

"I was just about to get you up. They are ready to move out and need to make sure everyone is on the same page, bro," Nick turned to walk toward the conference room. Dean walked over to Logan.

"Logan, can I talk to you for a minute?" Dean asked, looking at him.

"I will meet you in the room, bro," Nick said, walking away.

"Logan, I just wanted to let you know that those pictures do not tell the whole story. I saw a lot from the lens of the camera that I did not photograph, and I feel you need to know it. The woman in the picture put up a fight just before I took the photo of her standing in front of the window after the guy left. She just leveled the room, throwing stuff all over. The room looked like a twister hit it by the time she was leaning on the window, and that is when I took the picture. I just wanted you to know what I saw and that I would hate to get her on my bad side, okay?"

Logan put out his hand, Dean took it, and they gave each other a half hug.

"Thank you. I think I needed to hear that, and yes, she is one tough lady. In fact, the first time we met, she took me down and had me on my back without a second thought and walked away," Logan said.

"Yes, I read up on her and some of the things she has done, and all I can say is wow," Dean said as he turned and walked away. Logan felt better with this news from Dean, and somehow, it helped him to control the rage he was feeling. Logan walked into the conference room to get any updates and see about getting this plan going. He needed to find her and hold her in his arms and know she was safe. The meeting was short and to the point, and that was welcome news to Logan. They shortly were on their way as a group, and it was early in the morning before they were in their positions, as planned.

CHAPTER 13

TESSA WOKE UP TO THE SUN shining through the window. As she moved back, she felt a hard body next to her, and that was when she saw an arm around her. As she tried to roll onto her side, the arm pulled her closer to him, and she felt soft kisses on her neck. As she turned to look, she was pulled under him; one of his hands was on her face, and the other was around her waist, keeping her close to him.

"Good morning, gorgeous," James said just before he kissed her. His hand moved from her face, and he reached down to move gently over her breast. Tessa did not like this—in fact, it pissed her off. She could not remember getting into bed last night in the first place. She pushed him back before jumping from the bed, but when she stood, the room started spinning, and she had to grab the bed before she fell. She stood there nude, trying to keep her head from spinning. Feeling sick, she took off for the bathroom, and she reached it just before she emptied her stomach into the toilet. After throwing up several times, she felt better but still a little bit sick. She felt a cold cloth on the back of her neck.

"Sorry. I did not think it would hit you this bad," James said, holding a wet cold cloth against her neck. Tessa looked over her shoulder and saw a robe in his other hand. He handed it to her before leaving. She sat there for a bit, trying to get her head to work and to understand what he was talking about. The last thing she remembered was finishing dinner. She recalled nothing after that—until she had woken up with James next to her, naked.

She stood and started for the shower. She stepped in, and the water felt great. She could feel a slight pain between her legs. She stepped out, dried off, put the robe on, and walked into the living room. James was sitting there, drinking coffee and reading the paper. James turned when he heard her, and he then poured a cup of coffee for her. Tessa took it and walked to the window to look out, seeing only trees.

*　　*　　*

Logan had a camera and was able to look at her standing there at the window with a cup in her hand. She still looked black and blue, and her hair was wet; she must have just stepped out of the shower. Logan watched as James walked up behind her and tried to kiss her neck. She rolled her shoulders and sidestepped him. Logan smiled and thought, *Good girl. Still fighting, I see.* Logan watched as James tried again. This time, he was able to get his arms around her; he held her with one hand, and with the other, he grabbed her face and turned it so that he could kiss her. Logan watched as Tessa poured the coffee on James, and he saw James backhand her across her face. When her face came in view of the camera, Logan saw blood coming from her lip. James grabbed her again, but Tessa put up a fight. James threw her over his shoulder and walked toward a door. The curtains were shut in the next room, and from the plans, Logan knew it was the bedroom. Cold, hard fury started to build in his body, and it slowly moved through him before it hit his head. All he saw was red.

*　　*　　*

James threw her onto the bed, but just before he moved to try to cover her with his body, she was able to move to the other side of the large bed and was on her feet in a second. She was ready for him. James just layed there, looked up at her, and smiled.

"Sorry, sweetheart, for the slap, but the coffee was hot. You were much better last night. I really enjoyed myself; you are a wildcat in bed. I think it was around four o'clock in the morning before you would let me rest," James said, still smiling as he rolled onto his side. His pants showed how hard he was, but she couldn't care less about his problem and what he wanted. She did not remember what had happened and realized what he'd done.

"You motherfucker, you drugged me! That is why I was sick and dizzy. I should kick your balls up to your eyes for that. Why in the hell would you do that to me? Why?" She screamed the last word, looking at him. If she'd had a gun, she would have blown his brains all over the bed.

"Hey, it was the only way to get you into bed, and I will say that I loved each and every time you asked for more. Too bad you needed to be drugged. I would love to see what you would do without it. So would you like to try to see if you are just as much of a wildcat without the drugs?" James asked, getting to his knees to move to her side of the bed and closer to her.

"No, and if you even think of it again, I will grab you by the balls and squeeze them until they are crushed. Do you get me, asshole?" she said, moving away from him. She watched as he placed his hand over his junk. A look of pain crossed his face before a smiled replaced it.

"I understand, sweetheart. We have plenty of time. You will come around to my way of thinking. Trust me—it will be in your best interest to keep me happy and relaxed," James said, getting off the bed and moving toward the living room. "Oh, there are some clothes for you over there in the closet. Enjoy them, sweetheart." He walked out of the room.

Tessa walked into the closet and saw what he wanted her to wear. She thought, *no fucking way am I going to wear that in front of him. I can see through it.* She walked into the closet and found a T-shirt and sweatpants that she was able to make do with for now. She walked out into the living room only to run straight into James's chest. He reached out and grabbed her arms.

"This is not what I wanted you to wear. This does not please me, and that is the only thing you are here for if you want to continue to breathe, sweetheart," James said, and this time, the all-knowing smile was not in place. Instead, he was wearing an annoyed look.

"Too fucking bad. I am not here for your pleasure as much as you think. If that is the only thing between me and death, I will take death. You make me sick," she said, pulling out of his hands and taking several steps back so that she had space to move. If he wanted to find out just what she was made of, she was ready. James took a step toward her, and then someone knocked on the door.

"I am going to put an end to this and you!" he said, pointing at Tessa. "You are going to learn a lesson about doing what I say," James said. Then he turned to the door. "What?" A moment later, the door opened, and in walked a guard.

"What did I tell you? I was not to be disturbed!" James yelled at the guard.

"Yes, but there is a cop at the gate, saying something about an alarm that was reported here," the guard said.

"I will be back, and we will continue this. You had better think about it. I do not like this side of you, sweetheart," James said to Tessa, and he walked out the door. She heard the lock turn. She turned around and looked at the room, and she saw that someone had delivered the morning cart of food and forgotten to remove the knives. She ran over, grabbed one, and felt the beginning of a plan coming to her.

*   *   *

James walked downstairs to speak to the officer, keeping a smile on his face, when all he wanted to do was go back upstairs and teach her a lesson—one he would be happy to show her.

"Officer, sorry about this. I think someone is playing a trick on you. We do not have an alarm system with any company. We are just renting this place for a few months. I am here on business and really hate hotels," James said, looking at the officer and keeping his body relaxed.

"I am sorry about this, sir, but may I look around just to make sure that everything is okay so that my report is complete?" the officer asked. James did not know it, but the officer was really a CIA agent, and this ploy was a way of getting into the place and looking around. He had a small camera that was recording everything and relaying it back to the base camp a mile or so away.

"Officer, there is no need; we do not even have a system that would call out," James said, trying to get the officer to leave without creating a scene that would make the officer become concerned. If the officer started to poke his nose around, that would cause problems.

"Officer, this is my head security officer, Sid, and if there was a problem, he would know and report it to me, so you see, there is no problem here. Someone might have gotten the address wrong," James said, still smiling, hoping the officer would go the fuck away. He had other things he wanted to do now, and he did not want to stand there with a dumbass cop asking a bunch of fucking questions.

"So, Officer, are we good? I have some things I was in the middle of and would like to get back to—a business deal," James said, still keeping a relaxed body because he knew that officers were trained to spot when someone was trying to hide something.

"I would still like to walk around the grounds and take a look so that I can report that I did not find any problems. It will only take a few minutes. My partner will be with me." The CIA agent pointed to his partner, who was dressed as an LAPD officer. The first officer backed up and walked out the front door. All this time, the rest of the team had been getting into position and ready for the signal.

The CIA agents walked around the building, looking up at each window. They stopped under the windows of the room Tessa was in, and she could see them. She hit the glass, hoping to get their attention. Just when she thought they were moving away, one of them looked up and spotted her. Tessa waved her hands, trying to make them understand that she was in need of help. She did not hear James come in, but when he spotted her waving, it only took a few steps to get to her and move her away from the window.

"That is not a good idea, sweetheart, or I will need to kill them both," James said, wrapping his arms around her and pulling her away from the window. Tessa started to kick and twist, trying to get away from him.

She took a deep breath and stomped on his foot as hard as she could. James let her go, and she brought her elbow up and straight into his nose. An explosion of blood came out of his nose, and he covered it with his hands, leaning forward. Tessa brought her hand down in a fist to the back of his head, knocking him out.

Tessa ran to the window, but the officers were gone. She knew that the guards were still outside the door. Tessa tried to think of how to get the officers' attention. If she broke the window, the guards would hear it, and she could not go out the door. She looked around the room and spotted the phone that had fallen out of James's pocket. She picked it up and dialed 911. She hoped the call would go through. After a moment, an operator answered. She quickly told the operator that she had been kidnapped and that there were officers around the mansion. She was locked in an upstairs bedroom, and there were guards outside the door. The 911 operator was able to get the address and quickly contact the police to help and informed them of the situation.

The team had already contacted the LAPD police force to inform them about the situation, so when the operator contacted a patrol officer to look into the problem and the address, it came up on the scanner, and the team knew that something was happening inside. Logan asked the chief assigned to the team from the LAPD about the call, and when the chief called dispatch and talked to the supervisor on shift, he quickly explained the situation. Logan learned that the call had come from a woman who said she had been kidnapped. Logan whispered, "Fuck," and turned to Nick.

"Tessa called. She must have seen the cops out front and found a way to make a call. Glad we brought the LAPD in on this, or it would have been a shit storm."

Nick snickered and said, "Leave it to a woman to fuck up a good plan by trying to help get her rescued." Logan placed his hands on his hips, a slow smile came over his face, and he shook his head.

"Okay, I think that we should continue with the plan, but keep radio silent. If plans change, the order will come from base camp. Does everyone understand?" Logan said to the team B, which was going to the front. He turned and repeated the same thing to the A team, which was going through the back. Everyone nodded, and they all checked their gear and prepared to move out to meet at their spots, as planned.

*　　*　　*

Tessa quickly checked James, hoping he had a gun on him. As her hand moved on his back, she lifted his shirt and found a nine millimeter. A smile came across her face. "About fucking time something good happened," she said. She checked it to make sure it was loaded and chambered and took the safety off. She walked over to the window, looking for the officers, hoping they were at the front door. She looked left and then right. Not seeing anyone, she rushed to the bedroom, thinking she would get a better angle, but still, she saw no one. Someone knocked on the door, and moments later, it opened. She ducked behind the bed so she would not be seen.

"Oh shit, this is not good. Lock down the place—every door. If that bitch gets out, we are dead. Now, move," said the guard who had walked in and found James on the floor out cold. Two of the guards grabbed James under his arms, lifted him to the couch, lay him down, and gently slapped his face.

"Boss, hey, wake up. Boss," one guard said. James's eyes slowly opened, and he blinked several times.

"Oh fuck, my head is killing me," James said slowly, sitting up and looking around, trying to remember why his head hurt. "How is she?" James asked the guard looking at him.

"Do not know. All we found was you on the floor," the guard replied. "She did not get out through the door; my guys are out there and would have seen her," he said.

"Then she is still here in this suite. Find her—now!" James roared.

Tessa knew she was in trouble and trapped with no way to get out. She quickly ran to the door, stood by it, and waited for the guard to walk through it. Then she pointed the gun at his head.

"Drop it, asshole," she said. When the guard dropped his gun, she grabbed it. "Now move, and do not think for one minute that I will not blow your head off," she said, and she moved the gun toward the way she wanted him to go. She had his gun with her other hand and put her finger on the trigger. She'd been trained to use both hands for weapons. As the guard moved into the living room, James saw him out of the corner of his eye.

"Did you find her already?" James said, turning. He stood and found Tessa with a gun in her hand, pointed at the head of the guard.

"Sweetheart, you are not going to get out of here, so just give me my gun back. You know that there are several guards around the place, right?" James said, looking at her. Tessa pointed one gun at James, and with the gun at the guard's head, she pushed the guard to move.

"I'm not your fucking sweetheart, asshole, and I really do not care if there are a hundred. I called 911, and I will have backup here soon. Now sit the fuck down, and shut the hell up. I have had it with you and your games," Tessa said. Her eyes were cold and full of wrath, and her hand was steady.

James had read all about her and her training, skill with weapons, and black belts. She was a woman not to mess with, and he knew he was fucked if he could not get some help. If she got killed, oh well; it had been good for a bit.

"Do not even think about it. I will put a hole in both of your heads without a thought, so if I were you, I would just sit and shut up," she said. The door opened, and in walked two guards. Tessa still had her guns pointed at the heads of James and the guard.

"Drop them, boys, or your boss is a dead man, along with all of you," she said, and in a moment, she heard shouting in the hall and popping sounds. The guards turned and ran out the door. She heard gunfire. James started to stand up, and Tessa fired off a round into his knee.

"Told you to sit down and shut up. I will continue to put a bullet in you if you move again," she said, and she could see that the guard believed her. He sat down and relaxed.

"I am going to make you pay for that, bitch, and I will make sure it is slow and painful," James said between moans of pain.

"Cannot wait to see what you come up with, sweetheart," she said with a smile on her face.

CHAPTER 14

LOGAN'S TEAM TOOK THE FRONT DOOR, and at the same time Nick took the back, team two moved into the rear of the mansion. Logan wanted to have the element of surprise, so the teams were using silencers. The only sounds were from the cartel's guards. Logan wanted to push through and upstairs to find Tessa and make sure she was okay; the firefight did not take long. They quickly rounded up everyone and called in the LAPD to help cuff them as they continued to move through the mansion and clear out the rest of it. Logan was upstairs, and his team was moving from room to room, clearing each one.

Logan was the first one to open the door to James's room, where he saw a sight that took his breath away. There stood Tessa in a large T-shirt and sweats with a pistol in both hands; each one pointed at a different target. Logan used hand signals to tell the rest of the team to continue to clear the upstairs. Nick walked in behind Logan and just smiled.

"Well, I see you have everything under control and are not in any need of rescue," Nick said.

Two LAPD officers walked into cuff the guard and James, and one of the officers called in for an EMT to take care of James.

Tessa lowered her guns. She could feel her body shutting down, and the room started to go dark. Logan watched as her eye glazed over, and her body sagged. He was there in a few steps to catch her just as she fell. Logan picked her up and sat down with her on his lap; he was checking her out, making sure there were no wounds. His first thought was she had been shot. After checking her over, he did not find anything. He rubbed his thumb over her cheek and could see how bruised her face was. Her lip was healing.

The EMT walked in and first checked out James and loaded him up, but not before he was cuffed, read his rights, and moved downstairs. Another EMT worker moved over to check out Tessa. He needed her on the floor to be able to check her out. Logan had a hard time letting her go but knew she needed to be checked. The EMT could not find anything wrong but did say it might be a good idea to get her to the hospital for a thorough check. Logan thought that was a good idea and agreed. He watched as they loaded her up and took her, but not before he told them he was going too and would not leave her side.

The trip to the hospital did not take long, but the wait to find out what the doctors had found out about Tessa seemed to take forever. He did not move from her side. When they were through with the CT scan and x-rays, they moved her to a room and made her comfortable. They told Logan they needed to wait for her to wake up.

Tessa tried to wake up, but her body was heavy. She could hear voices but could not make out what they were saying. She knew this was not a dream, because she was not in the warehouse with her team. There was no one shooting at her. All she could see was a gray fog all around her. Tessa heard a voice again, only this time, she knew the voice. It sounded upset, and then there was a different voice, but she could not make any sense out of the words. They were talking about drugs. Then she thought she heard "no head injury," something about rape, and someone asking when she would wake up. Tessa wanted to scream that she was there and could hear them but could not open her eyes and see them. The thick gray fog rolled around her, and she could feel herself drifting with it.

Logan sat next to her. Nick tried to get him to leave, get something to eat, and take a walk to clear his mind. Logan said he was not leaving until she was awake, and he knew she would be okay. He sat next to her with her hand in his and his thumb rubbing the back of her hand. He would lean down, speak quietly in her ear, and ask her to wake up and talk to him, even if to tell him to go to hell or anything.

Tessa opened her eyes and blinked a few dozen times to clear them. The first thing she knew was that someone was holding her hand. She looked down to see Logan with his head on the bed, next to their hands. She knew he was sleeping by the slow, even breathing. She looked around and saw that she was in a hospital. She saw a blinking light and heard a beeping sound.

"Well, sunshine, it's about time you opened your eyes. My man here would not be able to take much more of you sleeping," Nick said, smiling at her. She turned to look at Logan and found herself looking into his beautiful eyes. It did not matter that they were bloodshot and had dark circles around them; to her, they were gorgeous.

"Hey" was all she was able to say, and the slow, sexy smile she loved and had been dreaming of spread across his face. He placed his hands on her face and placed a kiss on her lips, careful to not hurt her.

"Babe, I was so worried; you scared the shit out of me. When I saw the pictures of you at the window and your face so bruised, it just ripped me apart, babe, seeing you crying," he said, placing his forehead on hers and breathing in her fragrance.

Logan sat back and took her hand again, keeping one hand on the side of her face, just looking at her, glad to be able to look into her eyes.

The nurse walked in to check on her.

"Good—you are awake. I will let the doctor know, but first, I need to check some things, so if your visitors will leave, I can check you out," the nurse said, looking at Logan and Nick.

"I am not going anywhere, so you go ahead and do what you need to do, but Nick here can go get some coffee. Right, Nick?" Logan said, looking at Nick next to the door as Logan was standing next to the window with his arms cross over his chest.

"Sure, no problem, bro, be back soon," Nick said, walking out the door. The nurse kept looking at Logan.

"It's okay; he can stay. Besides, I really do not think you or anyone would be able to get him out of here without me," Tessa said, looking at Logan to see that gorgeous, sexy smile on his face.

"Damn right, babe. Okay, so do what you need. I will be right over here next to the window," Logan said, never taking his eyes off of her.

The nurse was not happy but took her temperature and checked her blood pressure and pulse, each time writing the information down and making notes.

"I will tell the doctor you are awake now," she said, and she walked out the door.

Tessa looked over at Logan, who was leaning on the window with his arms crossed over his chest, still smiling. She tried to sit up more, but Logan was there to take control of the bed, and he raised the head of the bed until she nodded.

He sat next to her on the bed, taking her hand and rubbing the back of it. He had many questions but did not know where to start. He did not want to upset her after everything she had gone through. Nick stepped in with a cup of coffee and handed it to Logan.

"So how are you feeling, sunshine? You had my man here worried. I've never seen him as single-minded as he was when trying to get to you. To see that you had it all under control, standing there holding not one but two guns—damn, sunshine, I was impressed. You sure have some skills, sunshine," Nick said. He took a sip of coffee and smiled.

"Nick, why the sunshine shit?" she asked.

"Hey, I am just saying that because my man here lights up thinking of you, so you must be shining pretty damn bright, I think," he said with a shit-eating grin on his face. She just shook her head but stopped when it hurt. A look of pain crossed her face. Logan stopped smiling, and a look of concern passed over his face.

"Babe, are you in pain?" he asked.

"Only when I move my head, but it's okay. I am fine," she said. Trying to reassure him that she was really okay, she wiggled her finger at him to come closer. When he came closer, she placed her hand on his face and pulled him in for a kiss.

"I am good. How about you, big boy?" she said softly with a wink.

"Oh, I am good. In fact, I am fucking fantastic, babe," Logan said, and that smile she loved so much lit up his face again.

"I think it's time for me to go. All this lovey shit is hard to watch. Catch you on the flip side, bro. Later, sunshine. Glad to see you are okay," Nick said with a wave, and then he was out the door and down the hall.

Logan turned back to Tessa and kissed her again. She opened her mouth, pulled his tongue in, and wrapped hers over his before pulling back and nipping his lips.

"Okay then, I can see you are okay, but if we do not stop that, the next person who walks in here might see more than they want. Besides, babe, I want to do it right the next time and have all the time in the world to enjoy. You understand me, babe?" he said, and she nodded and smiled.

"Oh, I understand completely, big boy, and I will hold you to it," she said. The door opened, and they both looked to see who walked in. They both started to laugh. For Logan, it was like music to be able to hear her laugh after everything she had been through.

The doctor explained that they'd found traces of drugs in her blood during the testing, and the doctor thought Tessa had blacked out just from the trauma she had been through. It was her body's way of dealing with the situation and letting her mind and bodywork through it. He also said that based on all the tests, there was no reason she could not be released. He informed her of things to look out for and said if she started to feel dizzy or confused, she should come back as soon as possible. With that, he turned and walked out. Tessa was glad to know that she was okay and able to get out; she hated hospitals.

"Good. I am so ready to get the hell out of here. So, what are we waiting for? Let's go," she said. All Logan did was smile and laugh.

"Babe, we need to wait for the paperwork and the doctor to sign you out. It might take a few hours; just relax. Besides, I need to find a hotel. I'm going to call Nick and see if he can take care of it. I think it would be best to rest for a few days just to be on the safe side," he said, stroking her face before leaning down to kiss her.

A few hours later, Nick was driving them to a hotel. He had booked a suite for a week. Logan wanted to make sure she was up to traveling, and he figured waiting a week might be a good idea, for her to rest and relax before they headed back. Logan had picked up a few things for her to wear, knowing she had no clothes. Tessa liked that fact that Logan had picked out simple things, such as jeans and T-shirts, for her. She was a bit surprised that he got her bra size right, plus the rest of the clothes' sizes.

Logan and Tessa walked into the hotel. He already had the key and room number, so he headed toward the elevators and hit the button for the seventeenth floor. The ride only took a few moments, and he took her hand and laced their fingers together as they walked down the hall to the last room. He slipped the key card through until a green light blinked, and he opened the door for her to go in. Tessa loved the view, but she was feeling a bit tired, and all she wanted to do was take a nap.

"I am going to lie down and take a nap, okay?" she said to Logan. He pulled her close and kissed her.

"Sure, babe. Are you feeling okay?"

She smiled and nodded. Then she turned and walked into a bedroom before stopping and turning.

"Hmm, which one?" she said, pointing to one and then the other. Logan pointed to the one she was about to walk up to. Logan had some calls to make and took this time to do so, knowing she was in the next room and safe. Logan was not happy that Joaquin had not been at the mansion and arrested. That meant he was still out there and a danger to the woman Logan loved and meant to protect.

Logan was on the phone with his office, going over something that needed to be taken care of. Nick walked in and walked over to pour a drink, looking around as if trying to find someone. Logan nodded at his bedroom. Nick nodded that he understood, and he sat down and relaxed, sipping on his drink. Logan finished his call, walked over to pour a drink too, and sat down in a chair across from Nick.

"So, any word on Joaquin? Do we have a location on him?" Logan asked. "I wish that the bastard had been there too. Then this shit would be all over, but now she still has a target on her back. She is not going to be out of my sight until that fucking bastard is caught or dead," Logan said. He took a sip, and just as he was about to say something, he heard Tessa scream. He was at the door in two steps, with Nick right behind him. Both had their guns out and were ready as Logan opened the door. He looked first left and then right before his eyes landed on her. She was in the middle of a nightmare. Logan replaced his gun, as did Nick.

"I will be out later. We might need to call in room service. I really do not think it would be wise for her to be out in public just yet," Logan said, and he shut the bedroom door, moved to the bed, lay next to her, pulled her into his arms, and quietly talked to her as he rubbed her back.

Tessa was deep in the nightmare, and it kept changing. She was having trouble keeping up, the dream kept changing, now her legs would not work, or she was moving in slow motion. At first, she watched her team being killed all over again. Next, she was running from James. She did not know which way was safe and kept screaming Logan's name. One minute she had a gun, and the next she did not. Tessa screamed Logan's name. She was scared for her life. She could feel Logan grab her and shake her, calling out her name, trying to get her to wake up. Tessa opened her eyes and looked into the eyes of the man she was trying to find. She wrapped her arms around his neck. She held on as if her life depended on it as a great sob escaped her. Tessa was shaking. Logan was worried and was about ready to call a doctor to see if they could get something to calm her down. Nick knocked on the door, and Logan yelled for him to come in. Nick looked worried.

"Is there anything I can help with?"

"Yes, call a doctor. I cannot get her to calm down—and hurry," Logan said, holding her tightly and talking softly. Nothing was working. A few minutes later, Nick and a man walked in. Nick said that the man was the hotel doctor who was on call. Logan explained what was going on and said he could not get her to calm down. "She has been like this for about 20 minutes. Is there anything you can do to help her?" Logan asked the doctor.

"Yes, I think I have something that will help, but I really need to know more about any drugs she might have had the last few days."

Logan explained, "She has not had anything from the hospital, but she was given ecstasy. That is the only drug we know of." He was still holding on to her and rocking her as she continued to cry. She had not let go of him; in fact, it felt as if she were trying to crawl into him. At times, it seemed she was not getting enough air. The doctor pulled out a syringe and filled it from a small bottle. He tapped it a few times before he leaned over and pulled her pants down on one hip to give her the shot.

"This will help to relax her and let her calm down. I will be on call all night; if you need me, just call down to the desk and ask for me," he said. After only a few moments, she started to relax, and Logan could feel her body go limp in his arms.

"Thanks, Doc. We will let you know if we need you. How long will she sleep with this?" Logan asked.

"About twelve hours or so, I would think; it depends on the individual. Like I said, I will be here tonight, and if you need me, I am still on call. I hope this helps her. Call me if you need to. I will let myself out," the doctor said. Nick moved aside to let the doctor by. Logan looked worried. He layed her down, covered her, brushed her hair out of her face, and kissed her forehead. Then he stood up and turned to walk out of the bedroom. Nick was already in the living room, pouring a drink for them both. He handed one to Logan.

"Do you want anything to eat? I could call it in and have them bring it up or go out for something. You really should eat; you will need to keep strong for her. I think she is going to really need you to be at the top of your game, bro," Nick said, looking worried. Logan was also worried. Watching someone, he loved who had been so strong and through so much lose control like that was hard.

"Yeah, I think we both need to eat. Order what you want. I can eat anything now, just not sure I will taste it much," Logan said, and Nick reached for the phone to place an order.

After both men finished dinner, they watched a game on TV. Logan kept an ear open in case Tessa needed him. He really was not watching the game; he did not even know who was playing or who was winning. It was getting late, so he said goodnight to Nick and walked into the bedroom and closed the door. Logan saw that she had not moved much from where he'd placed her. He walked into the bathroom to take a shower, and he heard her moan as he was drying off. He walked into the bedroom to see her moving her head back and forth. Logan threw the towel down, climbed into bed, pulled her close, wrapped his arms around her, kissed her, and talked softly to her. She calmed down and seemed to curl into him.

Logan woke up to the sun shining in. Tessa was draped over him with her head on his chest and her arm around him, and she was still sleeping. He placed his hand on her back and rubbed small circles. She moved closer to him and moaned. He kissed her and found that she was kissing him back. When he lifted his head, he saw that she was looking at him. Her eyes were clear. She smiled back at him, and he pushed her down, covered her, and kissed her again with all the passion and desire he was feeling and wanting to show her.

"Babe, why are you shaking?" Tessa said, pushing him back and looking at him.

"You scared the shit out of me last night." His eyes reflected worry.

"What about last night? I do not understand. I lay down for a nap—that is all I know. What happened?" she asked. She was a bit worried, not understanding why he was so worked up.

"You do not remember anything last night about the dream? You were holding on to me as if you would never let go. The doctor had to give you a shot to calm you down."

Tessa looked at him, and in the back of her mind, she remembered something about a dream—more like a nightmare she could not wake up from. She recalled him holding her, but she'd thought it was the dream. She shook her head, indicating that she did not know what he was talking about or why he was so upset.

"No, all I remember is a dream. I tried to wake up, and I was running and calling for you, but I could not find you. I thought that I'd lost you. I was so scared; it was so dark, and nothing made any sense." He could tell she was getting upset and could see the tears filling her eyes.

"Yes, you had a dream, but I could not get you to stop crying, even after 20 minutes, so we had the doctor give you something to calm you down. That was yesterday in the afternoon. You have been asleep all this time with me right beside you, holding you," Logan said, brushing her hair away from her face. Then he brushed his lips on hers and rolled over, taking her with him so that she was on top and looking down at him. She could feel how hard he was, and she rubbed her core over his rock-hard cock. His eyes became as dark as emerald, green with his desire for her. Tessa leaned down to kiss him, and at the same time, Logan flipped them so that he was on top. Neither broke the kiss, and each was giving all the passion and desire he or she felt for the other. Logan reached under her shirt and brushed under her breasts, and she moaned in his mouth. He rained kisses down her neck, wrapped his arms around her, and sat her up to take off her shirt and throw it behind him. Logan pulled down her bra straps and kissed the tops of her breasts before he unhooked her bra and threw it behind him. He laid her down and rained kisses down her throat to her nipples. Tessa moaned and arched her back, trying to push them into his mouth.

Hours later, they both lay there, covered in sweat and trying to calm their hearts. Logan jumped out of bed, picked her up, carried her to the bathroom, and turned the shower on. He stepped in, holding her close and raining kisses on her.

They both were drying off when a knock sounded at the door. Logan wrapped the towel around him, closed the bathroom door, and walked over to open the bedroom door to find Nick standing there.

"Bro, sorry about this, but I have news, and I really think you will want to hear it," Nick said, moving back. "Oh, you might want to get dressed, and by the way, how is she doing today?"

"Better. I think it was just a reaction to all the stuff. I think her brain was just overloaded, and it came out in her dream, and she had trouble separating them." He grabbed some clothes for himself, walked to the bathroom door, knocked, and opened it. She was standing there looking into the mirror. He walked over and pulled her back to his chest.

"Are you okay, babe?" he said, and she nodded and gave a small smile. "There are clothes for you on the bed. Get dressed, and come out when you are ready." He kissed the top of her head before he walked out of the room.

She watched him leave the room and then turned to look at herself. She had no makeup or hair brush there, so she tried to braid her hair as best as she could before leaving to find the clothes that Logan had talked about. She dressed quickly and opened the door to the main room, where she found not only Logan and Nick but also several other men, some sitting down and others standing, watching a screen. A few turned as she walked into the room. Logan turned around, reached out his hand for her to grab, and pulled her down onto his lap. There was a large flat-screen TV, and they were watching it.

"I am glad to see that you are okay, Marshal Miller and that you were not harmed," said the man on the screen. Tessa whipped her head to the TV and then looked at Logan.

"Sorry, sir, but she did not know that this was a video conference. Babe, this is the director of the CIA. He was my boss when I worked for the department. He was one of the many who helped to get you out of there and plan the mission," Logan said, not caring who knew that she was sitting on his lap.

"Thank you, sir, for helping to get me out of there," she said to the man on the screen.

The director reported on what they had been able to get out of the men who were arrested, but the one they really needed to talk to had not been apprehended, nor could they get any information from James about the location of his boss or any plans. James was not talking.

"I think I can get him talking. He has a thing for me," she said to Logan. He did not like the sound of that, especially after hearing that he had given her ecstasy. They still needed to talk about that.

"We can talk about that later," he said.

"Logan, I think that is a good idea. Make it happen—and do it soon. I think this meeting is over. If we need to, we can schedule a meeting later to update everyone," the man on the screen said just before the screen turned black. Logan was not happy that the director thought it was a good idea for Tessa to talk to James to see if she could get him to talk more. The rest of the group stood and walked toward the door. Only Logan, Tessa, and Nick were left.

CHAPTER 15

LOGAN LOOKED AT TESSA, THINKING SHE was so thin and should eat something.

"Babe, are you hungry? It's been a long time since you ate," Logan said. She had not felt hungry until Logan said something, and then her stomach growled.

"Yes, I am now. Do you want to go out and grab something?" she asked.

"No, just order room service for now. They really have great food—just ask Nick," Logan said, smiling at Nick.

Tessa had just placed the phone back when Logan came up behind her and hugged her. She lay her head back, feeling safe and cared for. A little bit later, someone knocked. As Tessa reached for the door, Nick stepped in front of her and shook his head. He looked through the peephole with his hand on the gun on his back before opening the door. After taking the room-service cart and thanking the staff, he shut the door and pushed the cart into the room. He looked everything over first before letting her take her plate of food to start eating.

Tessa did not know just how hungry she was until she looked at the plate and found that it was empty already. Logan just smiled at her. He was sitting on the couch, reading some papers. She needed to talk to him, and she knew that what she was going to say was something he would not like one bit.

"Hon, could I talk to you about something?"

Logan looked at her and saw fear in her eyes.

"Sure, babe, you can always talk to me about anything. Would you like a drink first?" he asked, knowing just by looking at her that she might need it. Tessa nodded, walked over to the couch, and sat down on the end.

"Hey, if you two need to talk, I can take a walk and give you some privacy," Nick said.

"No, Nick, I would like you here. When you hear this, you will understand why. Please sit down," she said.

Logan handed her the drink, and she gulped half of the glass before taking a deep breath and starting to tell them what had happened in the woods and how she had been taken. Logan was getting madder by the minute. Then she got to the part when James had drugged her. She could only tell them what James had said to her about it, because she did not remember. That was when Logan exploded, and Nick understood why she had wanted him there.

"I knew I should have killed the bastard the moment I set eyes on him! How in the fuck can he do that and feel good about it?" Logan was pacing back and forth, yelling about what he would do to James. With each step, he was getting worked up more. Tessa looked at Nick, and he nodded and understood.

"Bro, I think you need to calm down now and let her continue," Nick said, looking at Logan, trying to get him to understand that this was not helping her. Logan stopped and looked at Tessa. She had her head down, and he could tell she was crying. He could see how hard it was for her to tell him that she was raped. He sat down next to her, took her into his arms, lifted her onto his lap, and let her cry, kicking himself for being stupid and not thinking about how she must feel.

He wrapped her in his arms, holding her as she cried and hoping she would be able to stop crying, unlike last night. She was slowly calming down, and the tears stopped. She lifted her head, and he saw that the fear and worry were gone from her eyes.

Logan kissed her, placed her head on his shoulder, and just held her as he and Nick talked about what they'd learned about Joaquin. They'd been able to get information from some of the guards who were willing to make a deal. The topic of James was again talked about, and Tessa was better; she was able to get up and go wash her face. She poured a drink and sat next to Logan, leaning against him. Logan sat on the end of the couch and had one hand on the couch back and the other one on Tessa's thigh. They talked late into the night. Nick let Logan know she was asleep.

Logan said good night to Nick quietly and then picked Tessa up, carried her to the bedroom, closed the door, and walked over to the bed, which was not made. He laid her down and started to take off her clothes, knowing she would sleep better without them. He covered her up, stripped off his clothes, and joined her in the bed. Logan pulled her close and thought about what she had gone through so far without him. But he was there now.

Tessa woke up feeling good. There was some light coming in from the window, which told her that it was early yet. Logan was still sleeping next to her on his back. She quietly moved from the bed to go to the bathroom and started the shower. She stepped in and had her head under the spray, when she felt cold air and hands on her back. She turned to see him standing there, strong and sexy, with a wicked smile on his face. He picked up the soap and started to wash her back and kneed her muscles. They loved each other and enjoyed the time before they stepped out to dry off and get dressed.

Logan ordered breakfast for them, and they were enjoying a cup of coffee, when Nick walked out of his room with only a pair of boxers on, looking as if someone had run her hands through his hair.

"Sleep well, bro? By the look of it, I would think you have someone in there with you," Logan said, laughing.

"Ha, I wish. I have been busy. Thanks, bro,"

Tessa had a hard time keeping herself from laughing out loud, so she just kept her eyes downward and sipped her coffee. She watched as Nick poured a cup, walked back to his room, and shut the door.

"Is he always such a happy soul in the morning?" she asked Logan.

"Most of the time, but I am thinking he is in need of some R and R here very soon if you know what I mean," Logan said with a wink and a smile.

The CIA director called about what questions Tessa was going to ask James to see if she could get him to open up and talk more. They had been told that he had been transferred to the city jail and was no longer in the hospital.

Tessa used her deputy US marshal ID to get in to question him. She needed a room where he could see her and smell her but still be cuffed to a table. She walked in wearing a T-shirt, jeans, and her boots, looking every bit like the marshal she was. Her hair was braided and hung down her back, and she was wearing dark sunglasses. She kept a harsh look on her face, trying to keep all emotion from it. She needed to keep a cold, unfeeling air about her to get through this.

James watched her walk in. Many words rolled around his mind, including *strong* and *dangerous*, but the one that screamed in his head was *mine. She is gorgeous,* he thought, and he sat back, keeping a wicked smile on his face as she walked in and sat down. She removed the glasses and placed them on the top of her head.

How does one begin a conversation with the man who kidnapped, drugged, and raped you? she thought.

"Well, this is a pleasure, sweetheart. I have missed you," he said, leaning forward a bit and placing his hands on the table. Tessa lifted one foot and crossed it on her knee, keeping her hands folded on her lap.

"I wish I could say the same thing, but forgive me if I have no wish to be in the same room with someone like you, who kidnapped, drugged, and raped me," she said, keeping her face free of emotions.

Logan and Nick stood in a room down the hall, where they could see and hear everything that was going on in the room. Nick had to help keep Logan there, knowing how much Logan wanted to kill James for everything he had done to his woman, especially the rape.

As Logan watched, he was seeing the person he'd met weeks ago; she was strong, quiet, and in control. He watched as she started the questions, trying to get James to open up and give up the location of Joaquin. She did it by using James's feelings for her slowly. She'd been trained to get people comfortable to see if they would slip up and give out more information than they wanted.

"Why, James? I mean, at any time, you could have turned me over to Joaquin and been done with me, so why did you keep me? And if I should say so, you took good care of me besides the few hits and that slap," she said, pointing to her face.

"I am sorry about that, sweetheart. I just lost it. I never really meant to hurt you. All I wanted to do is love you."

Tessa was feeling uncomfortable with that statement.

"What made you think by kidnapping me and holding me against my will, I would return any feelings for you? Especially after you drugged and raped me? Just how is this going to work, James?" she said, hoping to prey on his feelings to get what she wanted out of him.

"After you killed Joaquin's son, he wanted you killed, so I started to read up on you. Through the research on you, I started to know that you are my match in every way and the mate I have been looking for. You are beautiful, skilled with many weapons, skilled in the arts, and one very tough lady. We took hundreds of pictures of you, from the time in the hospital to on the beach—even when you met him," James said with loathing, speaking about Logan. His face turned hard, and hatred shone in his eyes.

"You are mine. You should never have gone with him. I made a deal with Joaquin that if I found you, I could keep you for my payment, so the first night you were at the condo, I broke in and placed tracking devices on some of your things—ones that I knew you would always have on you, like your badge and cell phone. After I placed them, I walked over and knelt down to watch you. You were so lost in your pain. You had passed out, so I rubbed my thumb down on your face and told you how much I loved you and that soon we would be together. That was my mistake. I should have just picked you up and taken you then and not waited; it would have been better. Joaquin had a place where we could have been happy and safe. It was ready for us; all I needed to do was get you and take you there."

He seemed to be seeing all of this in his mind. He continued to talk about how much he enjoyed studying her and how impressed he was with all her skills. He told her of the many hours he'd followed her and watched over her. She asked about the place where they would have been safe—to see if she might have liked it, she said. James continued to talk about it and about the suite of rooms that would be just for them. She slowly moved him to talk about Joaquin, the places he might be now, and the possibility of her going to see this place that was just for them.

The more James talked, the more information he gave, and the more Tessa saw how crazy he was. He started to talk about the life they would have and the children they would be blessed with. She watched as his eyes clouded over, and he continued to talk about their life as if he were living it now. Tessa stood to go, and James's head came up. The quiet gentleman turned into a man filled with hatred and rage, and he started to scream that she was his and only his, no man would touch her, and he would kill anyone who did. She belonged to him and only him, and he was promised her if he followed orders. Tessa sat down again and asked him what he was talking about. "What orders?"

James told her that he would only tell her if she stayed with him, never leave him, and loved him just as much as he loved her. Tessa agreed to it, knowing that where he was going, she would not be there.

The whole story came out. James was the person who planned and followed through with all deals, and he was the one who'd told Joaquin to be at the warehouse for the meeting. He could not make it, as he was in Washington, DC, taking care of someone who did not feel that the information and support were needed anymore and wanted to stop giving it. When the name came out of that person, everyone in the other room let out the same word: *fuck*. Even Tessa was shocked at this information. The more that James talked and the information that he gave them they would have never in their wildest dreamed could they know that there was more to the story.

Logan turned to Nick and saw that he was thinking and planning already. Tessa stayed in the room for several hours, getting as much information as possible from James, hoping they could use it. When she walked out of the room, she was exhausted and was about ready to crash, when Logan walked up to her and wrapped an arm around her, giving her the support, she needed before she fell down.

They both walked out of the building with Nick close behind and then drove to the hotel. Tessa rested her head on Logan's shoulder and soon was asleep. When they reached the hotel, Logan tried to wake her up, but she was too tired, so Logan picked her up and carried her into the lobby. Nick had one of the staff park the SUV, and he follow behind Logan to help with the door at the suite.

After they entered, Logan walked to their bedroom to put her to bed. As he removed her clothes, he remembered what James had said about a tracking device on her badge. He removed her badge from her belt to better look at it when she was undressed, and then he covered her up and kissed her on the lips.

"Love you, babe," he said before picking up the badge and moving to the door. He turned around and looked at her, and his chest was tight.

He knew how much she had gone through, and he had not been there to protect her. He made a vow there and then that he would be her protector and would stand between her and anything that would hurt her.

Logan walked into the living room and found Nick pouring drinks. Logan turned the badge over and over, looking at it to see if he could find what James was talking about.

"Do you think that what James said is a load of shit, or do you think there is something there?" Nick said as he handed a glass to Logan.

"I was thinking the same thing, wondering if he is playing us, but if he is not, this problem just got bigger." Logan turned it over again and saw something. When he got a closer look, he found the first piece of the story, and he knew the rest was true.

"Found it. Take a look at this. I think we should turn this over to the boys in the crime lab; they might enjoy having a look at this." Logan showed Nick the small dot on her badge. He placed it on a piece of paper and put the paper in an envelope. Nick picked it up and walked to the door to deliver it to the crime lab at the CIA building. Logan sat down to think. With this new information, his thoughts were spinning. He sat there for about an hour. He heard her as she moaned from the bedroom. As he entered the room and closed the door, he saw that she was moving around. Her face showed pain and fear, and he knew she was starting to have a nightmare.

Logan undressed, climbed into bed, pulled her close, and held her; he could feel her heart racing and feel the tears on his chest as they fell. He continued to hold her, talk softly to her, and kiss her slowly until she started to relax in his arms, and he could tell she was no longer asleep. He looked down and into her eyes to see them shine with love, and he leaned down and kissed her. They made love for hours, enjoying each other and the passion they had for each other. Later, after both had showered and gotten dressed, they were hungry, and they stepped into the living room to find Nick and Dean talking. They were talking about the different missions they had been on and also the many women they had known, and they'd found that they knew and enjoyed some of the same ones.

"Ugh, you guys are pigs," Tessa said, moving to the couch with her drink.

"What? Are you telling me you have never sat around and talked about the different guys you have had with your friends?" Dean asked.

"No, I have not. Besides, I have no friends, only coworkers, and we never talked about that. Again, you are pigs—both of you," she said, pointing to Dean and Nick. All Logan did was laugh and shake his head.

"So, I thought that we might try the restaurant here in the hotel for a change, just to get out of this room," Logan said, looking at each of them.

"Sorry, big boy, but I am not going out looking like I just walked from the farm. I have nothing to wear there; besides, I really do not mind eating here," Tessa said, and a moment later, there was a knock at the door. Logan walked to it, opened it, took a package, walked back to her, and handed it to her.

"Babe, you now have something to wear," Logan said, smiling at her. She looked at the package and then up at him. She had a frown on her face.

"You had this all planned, correct? And what makes you even think that I will like this or wear it?" she said.

"Oh, you will wear it and like it—I am sure of it. Trust me, babe. I think I know you a bit more than you think. Now, go get ready," he said, pulling her up, giving her a quick kiss, and pushing her toward the bedroom. Logan turned to look at the guys, who had their mouths open.

"What is your problem? Never seen a man give a gift to his woman?" Logan asked.

"I thought that you really do not know what might piss her off and what she can and will do to you. I really do not think she likes to be manhandled after what James did to her. Bro, you are walking on thin ice with that one," Nick said, shaking his head but still smiling.

"I want you both there just in case if you know what I mean," Logan said, telling them both without saying a word that he thought there might still be someone out there after her.

"Logan, can you come here, please?" she said from behind closed doors. Logan walked into the room and shut the door behind him. When he looked at her, she took his breath away. There she stood, wearing the dress he had picked out for her; it was midcalf and molded her body perfectly, showing every dip and line of her figure. It showed off her breasts with off-the-shoulder sleeves, and the material was soft and moved with her every movement. The color of the dress was a deep blue that matched her eyes.

Logan was delighted that it looked even better on her than he'd thought it would. He smiled, walked up to her, took her braid out, and ran his hands through her hair, which curled around his hands and fell down her back in waves of brown and red. Logan leaned down and took her lips in a kiss filled with passion and love. When he stood back, her lips were swollen.

"Babe, you are gorgeous, and every man in the restaurant will want you, but I will know that you are all mine and no one else's," he said, rubbing her cheek with his thumb. "Did you need something?"

She turned around, and he saw her bare back and felt his pants get tight just by looking. "I need someone to zip me up, but if you cannot, I am sure that one of the pigs out there would be more than happy to help," she said as she turned her head and looked over her shoulder at him.

"No fucking way are they getting to look at this," he said, zipping up her dress. "Besides, it is all mine, and I do not share," he said, Logan kissed the back of her neck before taking her in his arms turning her around. He kissed her as he bent her backward with a hand on the back of her head and one around her waist. When he was done, stood her back up, and stood back a bit, her eyes were shining and were as dark as the deep blue sea. She stepped back to go into the bathroom to finish up, and Logan changed his clothes from jeans to black pants and a baby-blue button-up shirt. He put on a jacket over the shirt. Logan turned when he heard the door open, and there she stood, wearing four-inch heels that made her legs look longer and even sexier than they already were. Her hair curled and waved around her shoulders, and she walked toward him knowing just what she was doing. He groaned as she stood before him. He felt that she was the dream that any man would love to have, but she was his. He leaned down and kissed her.

"I really do not know how long I can keep my hands off of you tonight, babe—you are just stunning tonight," he said. Tessa smiled and reached up to wipe off the lipstick from his mouth.

"Thank you for the dress. I love it. So, are you ready to show me a good time, big boy?" she said with a wink before moving to the door and opening it. Logan adjusted himself before he followed her.

"She is going to pay for this later, and I am going to enjoy it," he said under his breath, smiling. As she entered the living room, both Nick and Dean gave out wolf whistles, getting a snarl from Logan in return.

"Just saying that the lady does look great, and those shoes make her legs even better, bro," Nick said, lifting his hands in surrender and laughing. Dean just smiled.

Both men had changed clothes, and all three were mouthwatering eye candy for any woman that night. They rode down in the elevator together and walked over to the restaurant. When Logan was asked if they had a reservation, he said, "Yes, a party of four under the name of McMullen." They were shown their table, which had a great view of the lights of LA. The food was perfect, as was the conversation. After a few drinks, Logan reached for her hand and asked her to join him on the dance floor. He pulled her up, walked onto the floor, and pulled her close with one arm around her waist and the other one holding her hand next to his heart. Tessa placed her arm around his neck and placed her head on his shoulder as they moved to the music. He had picked a slow tune so that he could hold her next to him. They moved as one to the music, and when she looked up at him, he kissed her; she moaned and pulled his neck closer. She could feel his desire against her hip.

"Babe, I think we need to go because I am having a hard time keeping my hands off of you now. Plus, I do not know how much longer I can wait to take that dress off of you and make love to you," he said, looking into her eyes.

"I agree with you, big boy, and I feel the same, so what are we waiting for?"

Logan stopped and walked them back to the table to let Nick and Dean know they were going back to the room and would see them later. Logan wrapped an arm around her and walked to the elevators and to their room. Logan kicked the door closed and wrapped his arms around her, lifting her up as she wrapped her legs around him. Logan walked them back to their room and kicked the bedroom door closed. Tessa slid down his body slowly. She lifted her lips from his and looked him in the eyes.

Logan started to unzip the back of her dress slowly, and as the dress fell off of her, he kissed her neck and shoulders. The dress pooled at her feet, and she stepped out of it and stood before him wearing only black lace panties and heels. She reached up to help unbutton his shirt and slowly pushed it off and let it fall to the floor. With a wicked smile, she reached for his belt and then his pants, but before she unzipped them, she rubbed slowly up and down, getting a growl from him. Logan grabbed her hands and walked them both back to the bed. When they reached it, he placed a knee on the bed and lowered her onto it with one arm around her waist and one on her neck.

He placed her hands above her head as he lowered his head and kissed her. It was a demanding kiss, speaking of passion and need. They made love for hours before both falling asleep.

She woke up with Logan wrapped around her; she felt protected, safe, and loved. After eating breakfast and having a few cups of coffee, Tessa was ready to see if any more information had come up and if they had been able to verify the information James had given them. The phone rang, and Logan answered it. After only a few moments, he turned and looked at Tessa with a look of disbelief before hanging up.

"What?" she said, knowing that it could not be good news, judging by the look on his face.

"That was the prison warden. James is dead. They found him in his cell. Looks like someone slit his throat."

"How did they know he talked to us, and why was he not watched better?" She was starting to get worried again. If they did not find out where Joaquin was, this might not end.

"There is one more thing," he said to her. "James left you a letter. They found it after they examined his room; it was hidden. They are bringing it over for you to read."

They waited for the letter to be delivered. She was interested in what he had written. A knock at the door brought her out of her thoughts. Logan had a gun in his hand and used the peephole before opening the door. A man handed him a large envelope before leaving. It was sealed with the one that the warden used. Logan opened it with a knife and took out the papers. Logan read one page, and when he was done, he pulled out an envelope that had Tessa's name written on it and handed it to her. Tessa opened the envelope and started to read, hearing James's voice as if he were there talking to her.

Tessa,

I know they are watching me, and they know that I talked to you. First of all, I want to let you know that I was never going to let Joaquin, have you. From the moment that I started to research you, I fell in love with you. You were too special to have Joaquin get his hands on you, and he would not have killed you outright; he would have made you suffer for a very long time. I know what you need and have detailed the information here for you so that you might be able to take the bastard down. I have very little time left, and just let me say that he has someone very high up in the CIA, so watch your backs. I was looking for a way out and was hoping that if I found it when you were with me, I would have taken you with me. I never wanted to hurt you, and I am sorry if I did. Take care, and please do not think ill of me. I have lived a long life, and some of it was not an honorable one.

Love, James

There was much more to the letter on the second page, including details about Joaquin, the homes he owned, the business he owned, and the names of his associates who were high up in each department. She handed the second page to Logan to read, and his face turned to stone-cold fury. He looked up, and anger burned within him when he read the first name on the list. Now he understood how they had known where they were all the time. He'd trusted that person. He'd looked up to him and thought of him as his mentor. How could he have been so blind? He passed the page to Nick. After he read it, several f-bombs came out of his mouth, and when Dean read it, the same words came out of his mouth, plus a few extra ones.

"We have a problem. If these names are correct, they already know what we are doing and looking into, and that gives Joaquin time to hide his assets and disappear," Logan said, looking at the other men. Their circle of resources had just been cut to only a fraction now.

Tessa was still looking at the letter; she was having trouble with what she read. James had tried to save her from Joaquin and the pain that monster was going to give her. Logan reached over, hooked his hand around her neck, and pulled her close. He kissed her on the forehead before pulling her close to his body.

"He wanted to save me from Joaquin. He knew what the bastard was going to do—and not just kill me. He knew they were going to kill him for talking to me about Joaquin," she said as she wrapped her arms around him. Logan enfolded her and felt her shudder. He nodded for the guys to leave, and then he felt his shirt become wet and knew she was crying. He pulled her closer and let her cry and know that he was there. He picked her up, carried her to the couch, and sat down with her on his lap. Her tears had slowed, and now only sobs were coming from her. Her head lifted, and he saw the strength he'd first seen in her eyes before all of this had happened.

"He cannot win. He needs to be taken down—and hard—to send a message to all the other bastards out there: the good guys always win, and the bad guys go to jail," she said with fury in her voice and steel in her will.

"We will, babe; we just need to come up with a plan now that we know about the leaks in the department, especially the main one, which I should have seen. Why else would they have known where we were all the time?"

A look of confusion crossed her face.

"The director is on the list that James gave you," he said with an edge to his voice. He pulled her down, and her head rested on his shoulder.

"If he is in on it, how are we going to make a move without him knowing? I mean, we are using some of the resources he has been giving us," she said.

Logan was not sure what to do or whom he could trust now besides those in the room with him. Logan was worried. He knew they were in danger now. Logan kissed her, stood up, picked up his phone, and made a call. Shortly after, both Nick and Dean walked in. Logan told them that as of now, they needed to go dark with the information they now had. They sat down and started to make plans until Tessa stopped them.

"What if they are listening or watching?" she said to Logan, close to his ear. He sat back, nodded, took her hand, and signaled for the rest to follow as they left the room and walked down the stairs. When they made it to the ground floor, they walked to a café to order something to drink and talk. They came up with a plan that would take them off the grid. When the plans were made, they returned to pack up and check out of the hotel.

CHAPTER 16

A MAN STOOD OFF IN THE shadows, watching and taking pictures. When the SUV left with the group in it, he jogged to a car and drove after them. The man made a call as he was following the SUV and reported that the mark was on the move and that he was following. He hung up and continued to drive. The man followed them to the airport and parked the car to follow on foot. He followed them to the part of the airport where most of the private jets were kept. He made a call about what he'd found and said he might not be able to follow them if they got on a private jet.

Logan had made a few calls on the way to the airport and had gotten a private jet so that they could not be tracked as easily. After they were in the air for a bit, Logan had the pilot change course. They landed at SeaTac and had a car waiting for them.

Logan had a place that was not in his name or his company's name where they could stay. It was off the beaten path, and it would be easy to watch for someone coming up the driveway. They stopped at the store to pick up supplies before heading up to the place. Tessa had thought it was a simple cabin in the woods, but what she saw when they drove up the driveway was a huge home that was made of rock and lumber. Logan drove into the garage to help hide the car. As they were getting out of the car, Tessa looked around and saw a five-car garage with only two cars in it besides the one they had come in. One was a pickup, and the other one was a Sno-Cat. *They must get a lot of snow up here,* she thought. They walked into the kitchen; it was large and looked like a cook's dream kitchen, all stainless steel. The kitchen looked out to a great room with a fireplace that covered the whole outer wall of the room. Looking down the hall toward the front of the home, she saw a large entryway with stairs to the right. She also saw a home office, a bathroom to one side of the hall, and a large closet.

Logan led them upstairs and told them to pick out a room. There were plenty—about six bedrooms, plus the master, which Logan was walking toward to place the bags down. Tessa walked into the room, which looked as if it could be someone's apartment; it was huge and had a deck off of it, with huge French doors and a view of the lake and trees. There looked to be no one close; she saw only the lake past the back lawn. She walked to the bathroom and found an oversized bathtub, a shower, and two sinks. There was a view from the oversized tub of the same lake and trees; it would be great for a romantic bath for two with lots of candles and a view of the lake. She felt him come up behind her, wrap his arms around her, and kiss the side of her neck.

"So, what do you say we try it out later, babe?" he said against her neck between kisses. She turned around, lifted her arms around his neck, and kissed him.

"I think that is a great idea. So glad I thought of it for us," she said, laughing between kisses. Just as the kisses were getting heated, a cough sounded from the doorway.

"Sorry, bro, but I think you might want to come downstairs and listen in on something," Nick said with a wink at Tessa before turning and walking out. "Oh, and by the way, I did knock. I guess you did not hear me," he said over his shoulder, walking out the door and laughing.

"One of these days, I am going to kick his ass," Logan said as he watched Nick walk away. Tessa placed her hand on the side of his head and turned it toward her.

"Why does it upset you so much? He is just joking with you, babe," she said, pulling him down for a kiss before letting him go. They walked downstairs together to hear what the news was. The news was on when they walked into the room. Nick and Dean were sitting in chairs, each with a beer in hand. Logan walked over to grab a beer and asked if Tessa wanted anything. She said yes, and they sat down on the couch to watch the news.

"Breaking news from Washington, DC. This story has just been released. A witness for the federal government was killed. The name is being withheld for security reasons, but the names of those who are wanted for questioning are ..."

As Tessa heard their names being said over the news, she looked at Logan. A look of fury washed over his face. Nick and Dean looked angry as well. Tessa could feel the cold fingers of fear running through her body. Her mind was running through what to do, whom she could talk to, and what resources she might have to help out. Tessa did not hear Logan call her until he placed a hand on her arm. She turned her head to look at him.

"I asked if you are okay. You do not look good, babe," he said.

"This is my fault. You all are in this because of me and what I did, and it is not fair. I need to talk to them and explain that you did nothing. This is a mistake," she said with a wave of her hand. "You all did not do what they are saying. They have it all wrong, and it is because of that damn fucking letter James wrote to me," she said, standing up and starting to pace back and forth. She gripped her glass so hard that it shattered in her hand. She did not even feel the glass as it cut her hand. Logan jumped up and grabbed a towel to wrap around her hand to stop the bleeding.

"Babe, stop. This is not anyone's fault, and we will get out of it. Let me look at this to see how badly you cut it." Logan took a look. When he took the towel off, the blood flowed down her hand. He rewrapped it and turned to Nick. "She needs stitches. Grab the kit. Babe, sit down, and look at me. You need to calm down and listen," Logan said to her, but Tessa was so far inside her head, trying to find a way to save these guys, that she did not hear him or care that she was bleeding badly. Logan looked at Dean, bewildered.

"Babe, listen to me: this is not your fault. None of this is." He tried again to make her understand, but all he got was her murmuring about it being her fault and her needing to fix it and save them all. Nick stepped back into the room with a bag and handed it to him.

"Bro, what the fuck is going on? It's like she is not even here."

"I do not know what is going on with her. But I need you to hold her down—both of you—so I can sew this up."

Dean took her legs, and Nick grabbed her shoulders and arms as Logan started to stitch the cuts up and stop the bleeding. He was concerned that she did not once yell in pain or look at him as he placed each stitch in her hand; all she did was talk softly of taking care of this and carrying out her plans.

Logan gave her a shot to make her sleep. As she fell asleep, Logan picked her up and carried her upstairs to the master bedroom. He said his goodnight to Nick and Dean over his shoulder and closed the door. He placed her on the bed, which was still a mess from their lovemaking earlier, and he took off her clothes and tucked her into bed. Then he took off his clothes, climbed in, pulled her over, and tucked her close with his arms around her. As he was holding her, he thought about why she might have reacted this way, and the only thing he could come up with was that this situation was like the case in which her whole team had died. It was like a flashback. Logan whispered into her ear, "I can help if you just let me in. I love you, and I want you always, and I will protect you. Please let me in."

Logan fell asleep with her tucked close to him, knowing that if he took his eyes off of her, she would run. Tessa opened her eyes to see a gray fog all around her. She turned slowly around, looking to see if there was anything there. A large figure came out of the fog toward her. As the figure came closer, she was able to make out that it was a man, and he looked like someone she knew. The figure walked slowly, as if it were hunting her. Her heart rate increased, and fear covered her body. She turned to run the other way, only to have another figure come out of the fog and walk toward her, as the first one had. Each time she turned to run, a figure was stalking toward her. She could feel her breathing increase, and the fight-or-flight response kicked in. Tessa heard a voice she knew calling for her. She turned around and spotted Logan on the ground with a figure over him. She screamed, "No!" and ran toward him, but an arm grabbed her and pulled her back. She twisted and turned, punching and kicking at anything she could hit. She heard a shot and looked over to see that Logan was on the ground with blood flowing over his chest, and the figure was laughing. The arms that were holding her disappeared, and she ran over, fell to her knees, and pulled his head into her lap. Tears flowed down her face as she saw the life-giving blood flow out of his chest and his eyes cloud over.

She leaned over and whispered, "I love you. Please do not go. I cannot live without you. Please stay with me. Please." She begged over and over. Logan woke to Tessa moaning and moving; he could tell she was in a nightmare and tried to wake her up, talking to her and shaking her. She started to kick and hit and screamed, "No!" She started to cry, and great sobs overtook her.

Logan heard her say, "I love you. Please do not go. I cannot live without you. Please stay with me. Please, Logan," and she threw her arms around him, pulled him close, and cried. He just held on to her and let her cry, hoping she would wake up soon. His heart grew three sizes when he heard her say that she loved him and could not live without him.

The next time he woke up, the sun was shining in, and he still had her in his arms. He looked down, placed a kiss on her head, and tightened his arms around her. Tessa felt safe and warm, and she snuggled down more as she slowly woke up. The smell of him filled her nose, and when she opened her eyes, she saw a wall of muscles and could feel his arms around her. Tessa lifted her head to look up at him. She looked into his eyes and saw love shining there.

"Good morning, beautiful. Slept well?" He kissed her forehead. She looked around, trying to remember how she had gotten there, and when she moved her hand, pain shot up her arm. She looked down to see a bandage on it and looked up at Logan.

"Do you remember anything from last night?" he asked, and she shook her head.

"I remember listening to the news. They think we were the ones who killed James, I think, and I cannot remember anything after that. What happened?" she asked, looking with alarm at him.

"You started saying that it was not fair, that we did not do anything, that it was your fault because of the letter from James, and that you were going to take care of it, and then the glass you were holding cracked in your hand and cut you really bad. I had to stitch it up, and you would not calm down, so I gave you a shot and tucked you into bed. You also had one of your dreams; only I think it was not the same, for some of the things you were doing, and yelling were different. Do you remember any of it?" he asked, hoping she would tell him that she loved him and never wanted him to leave her. She looked down and tried to remember; images came into her head like fog. She saw a figure, and then Logan was shot and dying in her arms. She looked up quickly, and a look of fear washed over her face.

"You were shot, and I could not stop it. I begged you not to leave, and…I said I love you," she said, looking uneasy, as if by saying it, she was giving up too much of her feelings, not knowing how he felt about her. She saw a look of pure joy and a smile that could have lit up a large city cover his face right before he leaned down and kissed her.

It was several hours before they came out of the bedroom and walked downstairs, where Nick and Dean were watching a game and eating a pizza. Logan and Tessa walked into the kitchen to see about something to eat and heard cheers and moans from the great room as the game continued.

Logan was preparing to make sandwiches when an alarm sounded. He looked over at the security system's panel and then walked into the home office and pushed a button. Several screens slowly came down from the ceiling. Both Nick and Dean walked into the room. Logan was at the computer, typing quickly as the screens came to life. They saw a vehicle driving up the driveway slowly, and when it stopped in front of the house, a man stepped out and looked around as a second man stepped from the other side of the vehicle.

Logan walked over to a wall and pushed a button, and the wall opened to show a large set of guns, from handguns to rifles to fully automatics. Logan took one, and Nick and Dean walked over, as each also took one. They walked to the door, and Logan told them to go out the back and around each corner of the house.

"Babe, I need you to grab a weapon and cover the front door downstairs." He kissed her quickly before running upstairs to a window that overlooked the front of the house. Tessa grabbed a gun and also a knife and stood to the side of the hall with a clear shot to the front door, making it a killing zone.

With Nick and Dean on each side of the house and Logan at the front upstairs, they were in good positions to take these guys out. Tessa was ready downstairs when she heard Logan's voice ask the intruders what they were doing there. She did not hear what they said, but Logan laughed and told them to walk to the door and walk in. Tessa stood ready, not knowing what was going on. She had her gun pointed straight at the front door and saw two large men walk in with their hands up, smiling.

She heard Logan run down the stairs and stand behind her, and she also saw both Dean and Nick walk up behind the guys.

"You did not think you could just drive up here without us knowing you are out there, did you? I think you are out of practice, my friends,"

Logan said, walking around her and toward the guys. He gave the men hugs, and then Nick did the same thing.

Both Tessa and Dean looked confused as to what was going on.

"Thank you for coming; we need the help, and you guys were at the top of my list. I would like you both to meet Tessa. She is a deputy US marshal and one hell of a good shot, and she's mine, so keep your paws off. This is Dean from the CIA. He works with IT and surveillance, and because he was with us when this shit went down, he is now part of the mess. Babe and Dean, meet Al—ex-military, good with planning—and this is Sam, ex-military shadow. I think that Dean and you might work well together Sam." Logan pulled Tessa close, with his arm around her and his hand resting on her hip.

Both men reached out and shook her hand and then Dean's. Everyone walked into the great room, and Logan asked if they wanted something to drink and told them to help themselves to the bar and kitchen.

"Just who are these guys, and why all the cat-and-mouse games in getting them into the house?" Tessa said with her hand on her hip, pissed off. Logan reached over, took the gun from her, and kissed her.

"I need to make sure that they were not followed, so when they walked into the house, a damping field would shut down any tracking devices and show us if they are being traced. I have worked with them and just wanted to make sure that they were not followed. We need them; they are not on the watch list, and they could help to check things out, since you, I and Dean are, if we show our faces, we are in trouble. It makes sense to have someone they are not looking for to be working for us to help find a way out of this shit and turn the tables and show the true facts," he said, pulling her close and getting ready to kiss her. She twisted her body and grabbed his arm and flipped him on his ass and left him looking up at her as she walked away. Tessa was pissed and knew that if she stayed one more second, Logan would be in a whole lot of trouble. She walked downstairs, where all the workout equipment was, plus a pool table and several other gaming machines.

She walked over to the mat, took off her shoes and socks, and stood there breathing for a few moments before she started to work on some exercises she used when she needed to warm up before practicing some jujutsu moves. Logan followed her downstairs and watched from the door as she moved through her exercises and then on to the jujutsu moves. She had also grabbed a pole, and she was using it like a weapon. He watched as she moved and kicked as if there were someone fighting her. She swung the pole down across the floor low, as if taking out someone's feet. She also used it to vault, as if getting to someone's back quickly. She jumped, flipped, and swung both feet and hands, flipping head over heels and standing with her back straight and the pole out to run through someone only she could see as she pushed it behind her.

This went on for about an hour before she slowed down and then bowed as if the person were in front of her. She replaced the pole and walked past Logan and upstairs to the master bedroom and into the bathroom. Logan followed. When he shut the door to the bedroom, he heard the shower on. He walked in to see her in the shower; he could not take his eyes off of her. She was stunning, standing there running her hands over her body as she washed herself. Logan started to walk to the shower, taking off his clothes, hoping to join her, when she spoke.

"You take one step in this shower, and you will find yourself on the floor. The door was shut for a reason. I do not want you in here, so get the hell out," she said to him without turning around and looking at him.

"Babe, what is the problem here? I can tell you are upset about something, and if you do not tell me, how am I to know how to fix it?" he said, moving closer. She finished and turned around, and with a motion of her hand and a swing of her foot, Logan was again on his back with a crack to the back of his head.

"I told you one more fucking step, and you would be on the floor. What part of the word *no* do you not understand?" she said, and she walked over him, grabbed a towel, and left the room to dry off. Logan slowly sat up, rubbing the back of his head where it had hit the floor and finding it painful. He walked into the room to find her pulling on jeans and a T-shirt. She turned and sat on the bed as she dried her hair.

"Okay, I get it; you are pissed. I'm just not sure about what, so if you could let me know, we can talk about it. Besides, I am tired of finding myself on the floor and looking up at you, babe," he said, walking closer to her.

"If I were you, I would go downstairs and stay the fuck away from me for the rest of the day, or you will find yourself again on the floor, but this time, you will be fucking knocked out," she said, her voice dripping with fury. Logan raised his hands, turned, and walked away from her. He went downstairs to join the guys, shaking his head and talking to himself.

"Hey, bro, trouble in paradise? I watched her take you down not just once but twice, so what did you do to her to piss her off that bad?" Nick said, smiling at him.

"I wish I knew. Not too sure why she is pissed off, but I guess giving her some space would be best, as she can and will kick my ass and everyone including yours too," he said, laughing.

CHAPTER 17

TESSA KNEW THERE WERE CAMERAS ALL around the place. She wished she knew where they were so that she could get out of there without them knowing or following her. She was mad at Logan for thinking she needed to be protected. She did not like that she did not remember the cut to her hand, which meant she was out of control and needed to pull back and start making plans and thinking more clearly.

Reacting with emotions was not going to work and would only make matters worse. She needed a plan—one she was working on alone without the apes downstairs. She cleaned up the room and bathroom, grabbed her clothes, and walked downstairs to use the washer and dryer. After a few hours, she had her clothes clean and folded and back in her backpack. She walked into the kitchen and was in the mood to cook. She looked at what they had and started cutting chicken and adding salt and pepper, preparing to make enchiladas. As she worked, getting the food ready for the oven, Nick walked in.

"Hey, that smells great. What is it?" he asked.

"Chicken enchiladas. I thought it would be good for dinner— something that is filling and that even you apes might like," she said.

"Ouch. Still pissed, I see, but do not take it out on all of us. Remember, I was not in on it, sunshine," he said to her, smiling. She just shook her head and continued getting dinner ready.

She called them to dinner about an hour later. She had plates, chips, and the chicken enchiladas out and ready for them to help themselves to.

Dean and Nick jumped right in and started to scoop up the enchiladas onto their plates just as Al and Sam walked in. They took plates, and each guy said thanks before walking back into the great room and sitting down in front of the flat-screen TV to watch a game. She was scooping some of the enchiladas onto her own plate when Logan walked in and placed a hand on her arm.

"Can I just say I am sorry, and can we sit down and talk about this?" he asked. She pulled her arm away and walked around to sit at the bar to eat. Logan grabbed a plate, filled it, and walked into the great room to eat with the guys. Tessa was still mad at him for treating her like a child. In the back of her mind, she understood why, but it did not make her feel better, though she did own some of the problems.

Tessa sat there thinking, *Where in the hell has that strong, independent woman I was before gone? I need to find her—and soon.* How had she become a female who leaned on a man, when in all the years she'd lived on her own, she had never once had to lean on anyone? Tessa finished eating and started to clean up the kitchen just as Nick walked in and told her that he would clean up. He told her the food was great and again thanked her for making dinner.

Tessa made a drink and walked outside to sit on the deck, watch the sunset, and enjoy the quiet of the outdoors. She sat there thinking and enjoying this time. She was so deep in her thoughts that she did not hear Logan walk up and sit down next to her with his own drink. They sat there for a bit, not talking, but the peace she had once enjoyed was gone with Logan there sitting next to her.

He sat there trying to think of a way to start a conversation with her to find out why she was pissed. He looked over to see that her glass was empty.

"Babe, would you like another drink?" he asked. Tessa handed over the glass without a word. Logan took the glass and walked back in to refill it with her favorite drink, rum, and coke, and then he walked back out and handed it to her.

"Okay, I have given you time and really would like to talk about what it is that is pissing you off," he said, sitting down and turning toward her, hoping she would take the hint. Tessa gulped half of the drink, seeking the courage to talk to him about this and try to get him to understand.

"Okay, here is what I see. You have been keeping things from me and treating me like a child, someone that needs to be protected," she said. She saw that he was about to speak, so she raised her hand to stop him from talking.

"I might be at fault to some degree with it, but I really do not like surprises, and today you chose to keep things from me about the guys that you called in to help. I understand that I have been leaning on you too much, and that is going to stop. You need to stop this alpha male shit with me and talk to me about your plans and let me in on them." She took a breath and a sip of her drink.

Logan leaned down on one knee next to her, took her face in his hands, kissed her, pulled back, and placed his forehead against hers.

"Babe, I love you and will do anything to keep you safe and out of harm's way. I get that you feel like I have been keeping things from you, and yes, I have, but it is not what you think. I have been working on my own, much like you, and found that telling someone my plans is just not something that comes to mind. If I am treating you like a child, then I am sorry, but, babe, I love you so much and just want to protect you. I will try to stop this alpha male shit, as you call it, and talk to you about the plans," he said, pulling away a bit and looking at her. Then he pulled her into his lap and gave her a toe-curling, body-melting kiss. Tessa melted against him and gave back the same toe-curling and body-melting kiss, running her hand over his chest and up to the back of his head to pull him closer.

"Babe, I think we should take this upstairs before one of them walks out here and sees more of you than I am comfortable with," he said, pulling her in for another kiss before picking her up to carry her upstairs. Tessa wiggled and pushed away from him. As she stood up, she smiled down at him before turning and walking inside and up the stairs toward the master bedroom.

Logan sat there trying to get himself under control before following her. When Logan walked in, she was on her knees with only a sheet pulled up to her chest and a leg showing from the side, telling him she was not wearing a thing. Logan shut the door and walked over, taking clothes off with each step, until he stood in front of her wearing only a smile.

The next morning, both Tessa and Logan were up early and found that the guys were still in bed, so she made breakfast for Logan and herself.

They relaxed over coffee until they heard someone coming down the stairs. They looked up to see Sam coming down wearing sweatpants and no shirt.

"Bro, do you think you could put on a shirt?" Logan said.

Sam just looked at him as if to say, "Are you nuts?"

"Coffee, Sam?" Tessa asked, picking up a cup. Sam nodded, and she handed him the cup and picked up her own to take a sip, looking over the rim at Logan as he continued to glare at Sam. Tessa punched him in the arm.

"Stop it, okay? Remember, we talked about this last night, and you said that you would stop treating me like a kid, right? So, knock the shit off."

Sam looked up and smiled, and then he turned and walked into the great room. A moment later, the other two guys came downstairs dressed in only shorts. They both poured some coffee and walked downstairs to work out. Sam followed them, and later, she could hear the sounds of a bag being punched and weights being used.

Logan walked into the home office to start up the computer and do some work. He had some things regarding his business that he needed to look at and take care of. He'd made sure to have a secure line that no one could trace back to him or the location. Tessa walked around picking up stuff and put a load of clothes and towels in the washer when an alarm rang. She looked up at the door of the home office, and Logan hit the button to show the cameras that are all over. What it showed was a woman walking up the driveway. Logan came out with a gun in hand and waved her over to the side. The other guys ran up the stairs, each with a gun in hand, and just like the last time, Nick and Dean took off outside to each corner of the house. Logan waved Sam to the upstairs window and told Al to stay downstairs. Logan waited for the knock at the front door he stepped to the door.

"Can I help you?" he asked.

"Hi. I really hate to bother you, but I am having car trouble and would like to use your phone to call a tow truck," a woman said.

"Sorry, but there is no tow truck in the area. Can I call someone to meet you by your car and give you a lift?" Logan said, not opening the door.

"I really am sorry to bother you, but could you just open the door so I could talk without yelling?"

Logan placed his gun in the back of his jeans and waved both Tessa and Al away from the front hall.

Logan opened the door and found an attractive woman standing there wearing a suit and heels, looking out of place. She was about five foot six, had blonde hair and gray eyes, and looked to be about twenty-five or so.

"Hi. I really do hate to bother you about this, but is there anyone in the area who could help me? My car just stopped running down the road, and there is no service in the area for my cell phone," she said as Logan let her in and shut the door.

"Sorry, but we're not from around here; we just rented this for our honeymoon. Babe!" Logan yelled down the hall, and Tessa walked down and stood next to him as he placed an arm around her waist.

"Oh my God, I am so very sorry; this was the only place close by I could see. If I could just use your phone and call someone to help, I will be out of here in a flash," the woman said. Logan saw Nick and Dean outside by the front door, looking and letting him know that there was no one besides the woman. Al was running a scan on her to see if he could find out who she was.

"What is your name? I am Sally, and my husband here is Ralph," Tessa said to the woman, smiling at her, trying to make her comfortable.

"Oh, how rude of me. My name is Beth. I am on my way to a meeting and made a wrong turn and found myself here with car trouble," she said. Nick took off running toward the road to check out the car and see if her story might be true. Dean stayed back, keeping out of sight. He would continue to have their backs if need be.

"I am so sorry that you are having problems. Here—you must be cold. Can I get you some coffee or something to warm you up?" Tessa said, taking hold of Beth's arm and leading her into the kitchen area.

"This is a great place, and I really am sorry to interrupt your honeymoon. I will be out of here just as soon as I can, and thanks—coffee would be great. Could I use your bathroom, please?" Beth asked.

"Sure, it is the third door on the right down the hall."

As the woman moved to the bathroom, Logan moved up to stand behind Tessa and quietly said into her ear, "Ralph? You really could not come up with anything better than that?" He then kissed her ear. Logan walked into the office to see if Al had been able to find out anything about the woman. Tessa waited in the kitchen for Beth to come out of the bathroom. Logan explained that there was a damping field around the house, so no cell phones would have a signal, and if the woman tried to get a call out, she would not be able to. The woman came out of the bathroom and into the kitchen. Tessa had a cup ready for her and asked if she needed anything else in it. Beth nodded for the cream.

"Ralph has gone to see if there might be anyone to help you with your car. So where do you work?" Tessa asked her.

"I work for a large PR firm in LA, and I am on my way to a customer to go over some of the things they would like to see on the company website and some ads too," Beth said before taking a sip of her coffee.

Logan stepped back into the kitchen next to Tessa, put his arm around her, kissed her on the side of her head, and whispered to her, "We think she is what she says she is, but she might need to stay here for the night until the information comes back with a full background check. Just follow my lead, babe." He stood up and looked at Beth.

"I cannot find anyone to help with your car, so I think it would be best if you stay the night here, and then we can see what we can find out to help you in the morning. I will let you know that I have some guys around here; they are our bodyguards. I am a man of great wealth, and this was the only way that my wife and I could have a honeymoon. We have a room available for you to stay in. I can get one of the bodyguards to go to your car and bring back any bag you might need," Logan said to Beth with his arm still around Tessa. Beth looked from Logan to Tessa, not sure what she was going to do. If there was no one to tow her car and no place to stay, then she was pretty much stuck there.

"I am so sorry for this. You are so very kind to let me stay here, and if you could get my bag, that would be great. Thank you," Beth said, still a bit unsure about this situation. What couple would let a stranger stay with them on their honeymoon?

"No problem. Nick would be happy to get it; just let him know which one, and he might need your keys if you locked it," Logan said with a nod behind Beth. She turned to see a gorgeous man who was six foot four and had blond hair and the looks of a Greek god. He was toned, tan, and sexy. She had not heard him enter, so when she turned around, she was a bit taken aback and slipped off of the stool she was sitting on. If Nick had not been there, she would have fallen. Nick put out his hand to keep Beth from falling off and to help her sit back on the stool. Beth saw that he had the bluest eyes she had ever seen, and the tattoo on his arm gave an air of mystery to him. He was wearing only sweatpants.

"Easy there, sweetheart. If you tell me which bag you might need, I would be happy to get it for you," he said, smiling at her and waiting for her to answer him.

"It is the gray one in the backseat and the small black bag too, please. Here are the keys to the car. Thank you," she said, handing over her keys and smiling at him, hoping she did not start drooling. She pushed her lips together and smiled again.

"Be right back with your bags," he said, and he walked out the door and down the driveway. Tessa watched the way Beth acted toward Nick and smiled, trying hard not to laugh. Logan also noticed the way she acted toward Nick, but he also was interested in the way Nick was acting.

"Okay, so I think I will show you to your room, and you can wash up or rest, whichever one you would like to do," Tessa said. She led Beth up the stairs and down the hall to the second door. She opened it, showed the room to Beth, and told her that towels were in the bathroom and that when she was ready, she should go ahead and come downstairs. Tessa left and walked downstairs just as Nick walked back in. Logan was telling the others about their guest and their fake names and cover story. It was important to keep up the act until they got the full report on Beth and found someone to fix her car.

Nick jogged upstairs with Beth's bags and knocked on the door. When she opened the door, she had her coat off and her hair down.

"Are these the bags you wanted?" Nick said, having a bit of trouble getting himself under control. It had been a long time since he had made love to a woman, and having this goddess in front of him was almost too much.

"Yes, thank you," she said, taking the bags.

Nick stood back and turned to leave, but before he left, he said, "Is there anything you need? I could get it for you—make you a sandwich or something." Beth smiled and shook her head. Nick walked backward and kept an eye on the door. When the door shut, he turned around and jogged downstairs to get a bottle of water.

"I tried to start the car. I think it is something with the ignition but will need to get someone to look at it to make sure. I am going downstairs for a workout if you need me," Nick said, grabbing a bottle of water and jogging downstairs. Logan and Tessa started laughing out loud, not caring if Nick heard or not.

Nick started off hitting the bag and then turned toward the weights as the sweat dripped off of him. With each weight that he lifted and each hit of the bag, he could not get Beth out of his head. Nick walked back to his room to shower and change clothes; he had a meeting with the guys to go over any information they might have on Joaquin and now Beth. Nick was the last one to the meeting. He closed the door and noticed that Tessa was not there. He raised his eyebrows.

"She is taking care of Beth so that we can talk without her walking in on this meeting. I will fill her in later," Logan said before getting down to the meeting and what little information they had on Joaquin.

"I am thinking that with the head of the CIA in the pocket of Joaquin, he will now be changing some of the locations of his operations and keeping away from most of his normal businesses and homes. What I have to report on the information about our guest is not good. She works for a PR company that is owned by a company that is owned by Joaquin. I am not too sure that she knows anything; all of her records are clean, and her income is not over the top for what someone in that position would make. She is in debt for about twenty-five thousand dollars and really does not have that much in the bank. She rents a small house. I would like us to be careful around her and to keep all conversations within this little play act we have been doing. What I am trying to say is that sitting around and watching games and drinking is not what a bodyguard would be doing. Guys, check out the area, and stay out of sight of our guest, okay?" Logan said, looking at all three men. Each one knew what Logan was asking him to do. The guys stood up and started to talk about what the plan was and who was going to do what and when. As they were walking out of the office, Logan spotted Tessa walking upstairs with Beth, asking her about her job, including how she liked it, what she did, and how long she had been with the company. Logan leaned against the doorframe and watched as Tessa continued to ask questions and make it sound like a friendly conversation of getting to know each other. He smiled, shook his head, and headed back into the office to work on some of the research he had done on the director and Joaquin, leaving Tessa to keep Beth company and try to get more information from her.

"So how long have you worked for this company?" Tessa asked her.

"Only for a year. I started out as an assistant, and now I have some accounts that I work on. This one I am going to is new, and I'd really hate to mess it up; they are a large account. I was told to make sure that I make them happy," she said before taking a sip of her coffee as the two women sat in front of the fireplace with a fire burning in it, warming up the room. The two women talked, and Tessa learned a great deal about her. As she learned more about Beth, she felt comfortable that Beth was who she said she was.

Tessa stood to make some lunch, and Beth asked if she needed any help. Tessa turned and looked at her for a moment and nodded, so both women walked to the kitchen to make lunch for the guys.

Logan was learning the same things about Beth, and with what he'd found, he also felt she was who she said she was; now he wanted to know why she would be working for a company that Joaquin owned and show up at their place.

Logan could not get the thought out of his head—something was not right about this. He did not believe in coincidences. Had the person they were looking to take down and hide from sent this woman here to spy on them? Logan was not ready to show his hand. Maybe she was innocent, and it was just by chance that she had shown up there. Logan knew there was a bigger problem he needed to work on: finding a way to keep them all safe and take the son of a bitch down.

"Logan, we might have a problem with the car. If it continues to sit there, it might bring attention to this road. I really think we should move it here and put it in the garage, and we might be able to look at it too," Nick said to Logan as he stood in front of the desk.

"Do you think you guys can get it here? I agree with you; it is just going to bring attention to us if we let it sit there, but first, do a sweep of it to make sure there are no bugs, okay?"

"Good idea. I will get some of the guys to help," Nick said, moving out of the office just as Tessa walked to the door to let them know lunch was done, if they wanted to eat. Logan stood up, walked over to her, and leaned down and kissed her on the neck.

"I like the sound of you as my wife and would love to talk to you about it later tonight as I make love to you," Logan said, and he then placed a kiss on her lips. He saw the shock on her face, plus something else he could not identify. Logan slapped her on the ass as he walked past her. Tessa was not sure what to make of his statement; she was still in shock and did not even feel the slap on her ass, but when she looked up to see the smirk on Nick's face, she punched him on the arm. Nick made a big deal of it hurting but never let the smirk come off his face.

The guys came up to grab plates of the sandwiches and potato salad Tessa and Beth had put together for them. After lunch, Nick had a few of the guys help him with the car. He first needed the keys from Beth, and as she was handing them to him, their fingers brushed, and he felt as if a light touch of electricity moved quickly through his body. By the way, Beth acted, he thought she felt it too.

With the help of the other guys, Nick was able to get the car up the long driveway and into the garage. He popped the hood and looked inside. Both Nick and Sam had been into cars when they were younger, and they both looked at it and found that there was a part that would need to be replaced. He had Sam go to town to see if he could find it. Tessa loved that the kitchen was stocked but was finding that they would need more stuff, so she walked to the office to talk to Logan about it. She stood at the door and watched him for a minute before he felt her there and looked up with a wicked smile on his face.

"Sorry, but that is not going to happen now. We have company, remember?" she said before stepping into the room and up to the desk.

"There is a lock on the door, babe, and it does work. Besides, this is our honeymoon, remember? So, it would not be a big surprise to find me with my arms around my wife and kissing her." He stood, walked around the desk, and stood in front of her, pulling her into his arms and kissing her until she melted into him. Tessa hated to end this moment, but this was not what she had come there for, so she pulled back to get some room between them.

"Down, tiger. Later, okay? I came here to talk to you about food; we are getting low on some things. I was thinking about steaks tonight and found we have none, so a food run would be nice," she said, moving away from him.

"No problem. Sam is in town now, trying to see if a part for Beth's car is in stock. I can text him a list; just let me know," he said before placing a kiss on her nose. She pulled out a sheet of paper, placed it on the desk, and turned to walk out. Before she was able to get two steps away, she was turned around and was pulled up against his chest with one of his hands on her neck and the other on her lower back. He pulled her close to him and kissed her slowly and hungrily before letting her go.

"Beast," she said as she walked out of the room.

She heard him say, "Yep, and I am all yours, sweetheart." Logan laughed at her. He turned to type out the list to Sam and asked him to pick up the stuff for Tessa.

Tessa had the steaks ready for the grill and asked if Logan would do the honor of grilling for her, but before Logan could take them, Nick stepped up and took the plate of steaks from her.

"Sorry, boss, but the last time you grilled steaks, they were overcooked from you not being able to take your eyes off your bride, so I think I will do the honors tonight. At least they will be done to perfection," he said, laughing as he took the plate and walked out to the back deck, where the grill was ready and hot. The sun was slowly setting. Tessa and Beth were getting everything else ready for dinner: baked potatoes, salads, and corn on the cob. They had set the table for everyone.

"Sally, I think it is great the way that your husband treats his staff, letting them sit at the table like this. They seem to be more like friends than employees," Beth said to Tessa.

"Yes, they have worked for him for a very long time, and they are more like family to us now," she said to Beth as Logan walked up and placed a kiss on her neck. Tessa called out that dinner was ready, and Nick placed the plate of steaks on the table and pulled out a chair for Beth before sitting down. The conversation around the table was easy and general, with some kidding toward each one of the guys. The phone in Logan's pants pocket started to vibrate. The phone was able to bypass the damping field that shut down all other phones. He took it out and looked at the number before making an excuse to leave the table to walk into his office and shut the door.

"Code Alpha 525 here," he said into the phone, and he waited for the person on the other side to give him the correct code back. When he heard, "Code Echo 1," he knew it was safe to talk and was glad to have someone to trust on the other end.

CHAPTER 18

SOMEPLACE IN THE JUNGLE OF SOUTH America, in a remote place, standing in an office of one of his many homes, Joaquin was talking to someone on a large flat-screen.

"I have given you enormous amounts of money to protect me and to find them, and now look at this shit in the paper. I do not need this shit in the paper now," Joaquin said to the CIA director, who appeared on the screen with a drink in his hand.

"I know that you wanted this taken care of, and I am doing it with what resources I have. You know I have to be careful now to not let anyone else in the department know what is going on. I understand that you are not happy about this, but it is good that the press is placing the blame on them for now. It takes it off of you. Let me find them and have them arrested for the crime. Stop worrying about it; this is good for us, and I have someone on the paper who can keep putting stories in it pointing toward them for the crime, so relax and enjoy," said the director of the CIA.

"I do not want her arrested; I want her brought to me. I have plans for her for what she did to my son. She needs to pay for that!" Joaquin roared at the director. The man was clearly anxious to get her. The director did not want to know what he had planned for her.

"I think that might be a problem. If they are arrested, and we take her someplace else, there will be problems with explaining the reason to the press," the director said, getting worried that if Joaquin kept pushing, all the plans he had in place were going to come undone. He felt the small amount of control he had on this slowly slipping away from him. He took a drink, enjoying the scotch that Joaquin had sent to him.

He had people looking for any trace of them and even had someone look into the company Logan had taken over after his father died. He hated to do this to Logan; he liked and respected him, but business was business, and he needed to pay for the care of his mother, the colleges that his three kids were in, and spousal support for his ex. He needed the money. Besides, he'd earned it with all the shit he'd had to take with the cutbacks. He had been working for the department for a long time, and the time he'd put in was the reason his marriage had broken up; he'd spent too much time at work and not enough with her. They should have been paying him more, and he'd earned this money by working with Joaquin to try to keep the body count down. Now it was all coming apart. He was trying to keep some control but found himself in the middle of a shit storm. He knew it was coming but could not see any way to stop it.

"I have every person looking for them and keeping all lines open in hopes Logan calls in looking for help. I know that he will call, and we will have him—trust me. Have I ever failed you? Just relax," he told Joaquin, knowing deep down that he was not going to stop Joaquin if he wanted to move without him. He had been doing his own research on Joaquin and found that he had many others he was paying who were just as powerful as, or more powerful than, he was. He was already making plans to cover his own ass with an offshore bank account.

"I hope you are not thinking of double-crossing me, my friend," said Joaquin with menace as he looked at the director. Joaquin knew that he had been checking on him and that there was an offshore bank account he was putting all of his money in. He could see the wheels turning in the director's head regarding how to make it out alive. The director looked at Joaquin. He had learned to control his face and not give away what he was thinking or feeling.

"What would make you think that? Besides, I think we have a good arrangement. Why should I do anything that would cause you or me a problem? That would not be too smart, right?" he said to Joaquin. Both men just looked at each other.

"Well, I need to get back to the office to see if there is any good news; I'll let you know if I find out anything," the director said, standing up and placing the glass on the table. He turned the screen off and walked to the door to get his coat from the butler, who was standing there waiting for him. He used a designated apartment for calls to Joaquin. Joaquin paid for the rent and the staff, so he knew that it was safe to go to. He walked outside to the waiting car and told the driver to take him to the office. As he sat there watching the traffic, his phone rang. He pulled it out of his coat pocket, checked the number, and saw that it was his ex-wife.

"Yes, Margret," he said into the phone as the car drove down the road.

*   *   *

"Ready for bed, sweetheart?" Logan said to Tessa, winking at everyone. They were sitting around talking and relaxing. Logan took Tessa's hand to help her up and wrapped an arm around her waist as they walked upstairs together.

"So why the act, and what is the hurry?" she asked as they made their way toward the master bedroom. Logan opened the door and placed a hand on her back as she walked into the room.

"I needed to talk to you, and besides, we need to keep up the act of being on a honeymoon and all that goes with it," he said, walking to her and pulling her into his arms. He kissed her, and she wrapped a leg around his hip as he walked them back toward the bed. He laid her down and covered her, continuing to kiss her.

"As much as I am having a great time with this and you, I still need to talk to you," he said, leaning up on his elbow and seeing that dreamy look she got when desire took over.

"First you tell me we need to go to bed, then you kiss me to the point where I am ready to take your clothes off, and now you tell me we need to talk. This is not going well for you to get anything later, babe," she said to him, smiling.

"Yeah, I can see that, but it is important that we talk. I need to know what you found out about her and to see if the information is the same as what we were able to find out. I was able to find out that there really is nothing about her that screams she is anything but what she says. So, what did you find out from your little girl talk?" he said to her as he moved next to her, putting his head on his hand and looking at her, waiting for her to explain what they'd talked about.

She told him, "Beth is from a large family from Texas. Her father is a lawyer, and her mom stays at home. She has one older brother and two younger sisters. She finished college there at Texas and was in several different jobs before she was hired at the PR firm. She has only been on the job for less than a year and just moved up to the position she is in now." After Tessa told him everything she had been able to get out of Beth, they found that their information matched. However, he was still uncomfortable about the whole thing. It seemed too good to be true.

Afterward, they talked more about it to see if there was any other way to find out if she was really who she said she was without breaking their cover. Then they continued their lovemaking, and she made him work for it.

The sun was shining in from the window. As Tessa opened her eyes, she could feel a solid wall of muscle behind her and an arm around her. As she tried to move, the arm pulled her back tightly against him as he kissed her neck down to her shoulder, moving his hand up at the same time. She rolled over to face him. Tessa kissed him back, and before they knew it, they'd spent hours in bed. Then they took a shower, and it was midmorning when they both walked downstairs.

Beth was sitting at the bar, drinking coffee and reading a paper, and Nick was sitting on the couch, watching the news. Logan looked over to see breaking news come across the screen with their pictures. Nick quickly turned the channel and looked back at Logan; his eyes clearly showed concern that their faces were all over the news.

It looked as if the director was getting anxious to find them. For now, only the four of them were wanted; they did not know about Al and Sam, so they would be the ones to do anything in town for now. Logan had not been able to talk to them about the code Echo 1 from the call. He needed to talk to them about it to see what kind of plan they could come up with to clear themselves, put the light back on Joaquin and the director, and show just how high up the corruption had gone. Tessa walked up to Beth and asked her if she'd slept well, trying to keep Beth's attention on her and not the guys. Logan leaned down to tell Nick, "Meeting in thirty minutes. Tell the guys too." Logan walked over to get a cup of coffee and to tell Tessa that he would be busy with the guys in the office and that she should stay inside and keep the doors locked. He kissed her and took his coffee into the office, shutting the door.

Logan walked to the desk and started up the computer and the flat screen to show the guys what he had so far. He opened the desk and unlocked a safe inside of it to take out the file he had been working on and needed to show the guys. He would ask them if they have any ideas for a plan that would get them all out of this mess.

The door to the office opened thirty minutes later and in walked the guys. Each took a seat at the long table in the office. Logan placed a file on the desk, and a few pictures fell out. The guys each took a turn looking at them. Logan explained that he'd made the call and that the code Echo 1 had come back for them. This was great news; it meant that they had friends out there who understood that they needed help to shut down the leak in the CIA and take the director out. He asked Al and Sam if they wanted to walk and said he would understand now that the news was showing his, Tessa's, Dean's, and Nick's pictures. The guys shook their heads and said they had his back. Logan took a breath; he had not been sure they would want to stay once the news started showing their pictures.

So, they worked on coming up with a plan. Logan called Tessa on the phone to ask if she would make some sandwiches and coffee and bring in a case of bottled water. They worked through the day and late into the night with only a few breaks to eat or take a walk. Tessa made sure they had food and drinks, and she kept Beth busy with other things. They had laundry to do, and Tessa wanted to take all the bedding off and put fresh sheets on. All the work she wanted to do kept her and Beth busy most of the day and away from the TV and any news that might come on. It was late, so they each had a drink, and she put a movie in so that there would be no way for the news to break in and show their faces.

It was close to midnight when the office door opened, and the guys came out. Each one walked off to his room, but before they made it far, Tessa told them what she and Beth had done. Each one thanked them and continued to his room to shower and take a watch if scheduled or, if he had the night off, to go to sleep. Logan walked over and asked Tessa if she was ready to go to bed because he sure was.

Beth had already stood up and was walking upstairs to go to bed herself. Tessa turned the TV off and walked upstairs with Logan with their arms around each other. They walked into their room and shut the door, shutting out the world out so that they could be alone to love each other over and over throughout the night.

* * *

"I told you to let me know anytime there is any information on them and not to release it to the press. Why in the hell did that get released without my okay on it?" the director yelled at the assistant standing there, who did not know how the information had been released and or who had done it.

"Yes, sir, I will find out and let you know. I have no idea who released it, but I will find out. Sorry, sir," she said, backing out of the office as quickly as she could and closing the door. She moved to her desk and placed a call.

"Code 525, the mail is here," she said into the phone, and then she hung up and continued to type a letter for the director.

Somewhere in a different part of the building, a person was placing a call."Echo 1," the caller said before replacing the phone and continuing to work on paperwork.

* * *

As Logan was getting ready to go to sleep, the phone rang. As he looked at the screen and saw a name, he answered it.

"Code 525," he said.

He heard, "Echo 1," and the line went dead. Logan could feel the smile spread across his face, knowing that the time was close when they would be safe. Tessa would be safe, and that was all he really cared about. He lay back down and pulled her close to him, knowing she was safe there in his arms and would be safe from all of this soon. After the threat to them was gone, he planned on keeping her safe in his arms for the rest of their lives. As he fell asleep, he pictured marrying her and loving her. He fell asleep with a smile on his face.

Nick was up early, knowing he had to get Beth's car done and get her out of there today if at all possible. Al found him with his head under the hood of her car, finishing up the job; he had just tightened the last bolt. Nick told Al to reach in and start it. As Al turned the key, the motor roared to life, and the guys high-fived. Nick wiped down the sides of the car, and anyplace he might have touched, shut the hood, and turned the key to shut the motor off. As Nick was walking back into the kitchen to wash up, he just about ran Beth over. He had to grab her to keep her from falling over.

"Shit, sorry. I did not see you there. Are you all right?" he asked her, helping her stand up as she lifted her eyes to look at him. She could feel the sparks all over her body; where he touched her left a tingling on her skin. He made sure she was able to stand on her own and then bent down and placed his finger under her chin to lift it up.

"Are you sure you are all right? You look a little pale. Shit, I am so sorry. Here—let me help you sit down. Come over here, and take this chair. Can I get you a glass of water or something? Fuck, I am covered in grease and getting it all over you. Here—let me get cleaned up, and I will get that glass for you. Just sit still." He walked over to the sink to clean up and scrubbed his hands and arms any place he saw grease. After he made sure he was cleaned up, he took a wet, soapy cloth over to her to clean her arm where he had touched her. He also filled up a glass of water for her. As Nick cleaned the grease from her arms, he kept looking up at her from under his eyelashes to see if her color was coming back.

"Drink the water; it might help. You are still pale," he said. Beth thought the only thing that would help was feeling his arms around her and his lips moving over her's. She wanted to know how his body would feel next to her's. She could feel her body heat up and knew she was blushing. She lowered her head and hoped he would not see it. As Nick looked up and saw her head lowered, he got worried, and he again placed his finger under her chin to lift her head to look into her face.

"Hey, are you sure you are okay? Are you sure that I did not hurt you? Well, you seem to have some color back in your face; that is a good sign," Nick said, seeing a blush cover her face. With the way her head was down, he knew she did not want him to see it, so he coughed, handed her the cloth to finish up the job, and started to walk away. He was halfway up the stairs, when he remembered that her car was fixed.

"Shit, sorry. Did not mean to scare you again," he said when he watched her jump. "I was able to fix your car, and it is running fine now." He turned to walk upstairs and heard a small voice come from her.

"Thank you," she said.

He stopped and turned to say, "You are welcome," and continued upstairs to clean up more, and to let Logan know the car was done and working, and see what he would like to do about it.

Logan was walking out of his room. As he closed the door, Nick walked up to tell him the car was fixed. All Logan said was "Good," and he walked downstairs.

"Nick just told me that your car is fixed, so does that mean you will be leaving in the morning? That way, you will have a fresh day to start. I will see about getting you the directions to get where you were going, okay?" Logan said to Beth, and he walked into his office. The only thing Beth was thinking about was the way Nick made her feel. She smiled, wishing she did not need to go. She would like to get to know him more, but she knew she needed to get back on the road to make it to the appointment on time. If she left in the morning, she would make it, as long as she did not get lost again.

Nick stepped into the shower and made sure it was cold to help with his desire and to help him cool off. He washed, rinsed off, and stepped out to dry off as quickly as he could, as the water was cold. Nick grabbed a pair of jeans, slipped them on, pulled a T-shirt over his head, raked his fingers through his hair, and walked out into the hall to go downstairs to grab a beer and see what might be for dinner. Tessa had made some great dishes, and it was great to know that at least someone there knew how to cook. As Nick reached the bottom of the stairs, he could smell something wonderful coming from the kitchen. As he walked in to get a better smell, he spotted Beth at the stove, and he could not see Tessa.

"So, what is for dinner today? It smells great," Nick said.

Beth turned around. She could not understand how someone that gorgeous would look at her. She cleared her throat. "I am cooking today, letting Sally off for the night. It is a dish from my grandmother. I just hope everyone likes it." She turned quickly to keep him from seeing the blush covering her face.

Nick pushed off the counter and moved to the wet bar for a beer. As he grabbed a beer, he heard the rest of the guys moving toward the bar, so Nick stepped behind to play bartender, asking them what they wanted, mixing it, and passing it to them. As he watched Tessa come up from downstairs and walk toward the bar, he started her drink, knowing without being told what she liked. As Tessa stood next to the bar, a glass was pushed in front of her, and Nick leaned over to her.

"The guy at the end of the bar would like to buy you a drink, miss," he said, and he winked. Tessa laughed and looked to see Logan standing there with a smile on his face, and he lifted one eyebrow at her. Al had scotch, and Logan, Sam, and Dean each had a beer.

"Beth, can I get you anything from the bar? The guy at the end is buying," Nick said with a wink at her.

"Sure, white wine if you have any. Thank you," she said before turning toward the stove to look into a pot. Nick poured her a glass of wine, walked it over to her, and placed it on the counter within her reach.

"Here you go, and it's on the house." Nick turned to walk back to the bar to finish his beer.

"Hey, can I help you set the table? It is the least I can do to help since you would not let me help you with dinner. And maybe the guys can do the dishes—right, guys?" Tessa said, turning to wink over her shoulder at the guys. They all said it was no problem.

After Tessa and Beth had the table set, Beth said that dinner was ready and watched as Nick walked up to pull out her chair for her before sitting down next to her. They all filled their plates, and she could hear the sounds of happy people eating and thanking her for the great dinner.

She was having trouble eating with Nick sitting next to her. She knew that the food was great, but she did not taste it. When dinner was over, the guys told the girls to go relax; they would take care of the cleanup. So, Beth and Tessa sat down and talk until the guys came over to refill their glasses and join the girls. They talked for a long time, and friendly insults were thrown back and forth among some of the guys. What seemed like a few minutes turned into hours, and Beth could feel her eyes getting heavy. She yawned, said goodnight to everyone, and walked upstairs to her room to get ready for bed, hoping she could sleep and stop thinking of Nick.

After Beth was upstairs, they were free to talk more openly about things. Logan told them he'd been able to get directions to the place she was going, and he'd also put tracking devices on her car and in her purse. The one in her purse also was a listening device. He told them about the call late last night, and he could see that everyone was ecstatic at the good news.

With the mission planning the guys had done a few days ago and the information Logan had been able to get from his source, they were close to getting their names cleared. They only needed a few more things to fall into place, and the trap would be set. They were hoping to catch the big fucking mouse and all the little mice too. They would blow the lid off everything, and they made sure they had proof that they'd been set up to take the fall.

The first part was to get Beth out of there and on her way with the devices they'd placed on her to help listen and track her. The next thing was to carefully leak stories about some things that would not look good for the director, and that would start the ball for the investigation. Logan knew someone in the investigating department, and he had mailed an envelope to him with plenty of information that would prove the director was dirty and show where all the skeletons were hidden. Logan knew more than the director thought he did, and that would help everything fall into place as soon as the package was delivered.

As they looked at each other with smiles, they lifted their glasses and clinked them together. Tessa had a surprise too: some connections the director didn't know about that had helped to prove they'd been set up. After they all finished their drinks, they made their way to their rooms to rest for the bomb that was about to go off.

Tessa knew they had everything in place to show the public the truth, but she was still nervous about it. After she had brushed her teeth she was scrubbing her face and getting ready for bed; Logan was watching her. She was deep in thought and did not even see herself in the mirror as she was scrubbing her face. He watched her go through the routine she did each night.

"Babe?" he said. When she did not respond, he came up behind her, placed his hands on her shoulders, looked at her in the mirror, and said, "Babe, you have scrubbed your face to the point that you are turning red. What is going on inside your head? Talk to me. I am right here and listening to you." He slowly turned her around to look at her in the face. Tessa looked up and saw understanding and love shining from his eyes as they looked down at her. She took a deep breath, let it out, wrapped her arms around him, and hugged him tightly.

"I am scared that if just one part does not work, we will have a problem. I am just waiting for the other shoe to drop is all, and I just hope that no one will get hurt through this," she said, lifting her face to look up at him. She could see the concern on his face for her. Logan leaned down to kiss her, lifted her up, carried her to the bed, slowly lowered her down, and covered her without breaking the kiss, showing her how much he loved her.

It was several hours before they fell asleep, and Tessa woke up early in the morning to the smell of coffee and the sounds of voices.

Nick was yelling at Logan, and the other guys were trying to get them to stop yelling and listen to each other. Tessa walked between them, putting a hand on each of their chests, and pushed back and yelled for them to stop. Both stopped and looked down at her.

"Okay, so what the hell is the pissing contest all about now?" she asked.

"Beth is gone, and I wanted her to wait to go, but fucking boss man here gave her the information on how to get there, so she left a note, and I just think it is chickenshit that he is using her this way," Nick said, looking straight at Logan, fuming.

"Hey, I never told her to leave before anyone was up, and you were in the meeting about what we were doing with her and did not say a fucking thing about it, so what the hell has your panties in a twist, bro?" Logan shouted. Tessa knew what was going on, and they were both being asses.

"Hey, stop yelling, and talk to me, okay? Logan is right; you signed off on the plan with her. Nick is right too; it is shitty to use her that way without letting her know anything. I am also worried about it and tried to talk to you last night about it," she told them, looking first at Nick and then at Logan. "But it really does not matter now. She is gone."

CHAPTER 19

"BABE, WHAT THE HELL ARE YOU smiling at? Eat! We have a lot going on," Logan said.

Tessa filled her plate and started to eat, thinking, *Yes, a lot is going to be happening here very soon. Justice will soon come full circle, and all the men and women who were killed by Joaquin will be put to rest.*

* * *

At the same time, the head of the FBI was handed a large envelope to open. Out came a CD, several pictures, a detailed list of locations, and a letter informing him that the same information had been delivered to several different departments and the major news stations. The director of the FBI put the CD in and hit the start button. What he saw and heard immediately grabbed his attention, and he stopped the footage. He called a meeting and also put a call into each one of the departments listed in the letter. If this information was true and the news stations ran it, all hell was going to break loose.

"Sir, I have the head of the justice department on line two for you; he wants to speak to you now," said his assistant. As the director took the call, he heard a noise coming from behind his door. The door opened, and there stood several deputy US marshals.

One said, "Sir, I am here to inform you that you are under arrest. You have the right to remain silent. If you say anything, it can be used against you in a court of law. You have the right to have an attorney present during any questioning. If you cannot afford an attorney, one will be appointed for you if you so desire. Do you understand your rights, sir? Would you like to make a statement?" They placed handcuffs over his wrists and led him out the door and down to the elevator.

The director of the CIA was being led down the hall with two large deputy US marshals on each side of him. Just like the director of the FBI both were on Joaquin's payroll and the CD had the information on it to prove it. The Department of Justice was given the same CD, and they had a warrant out for their arrest. As each department head was led off in handcuffs. Was justice served, only time will tell, but not until each and every one of those that play a part in this was sentenced to prison. Than and only than will the circle of justice come full circle and the left hand of Justice would than be served.

*   *   *

At the same time, at different locations listed on the papers sent to the different places, arrests were being made. Joaquin was placed under arrest and put in a cell, along with many of the other people named in the papers. A full investigation was ordered from the White House and down through the different departments. Each department was going to be under investigation because of the leak of information.

*   *   *

Logan was waiting by the phone in his office as the guys were watching the TV for any news that the trap had been opened. Logan was standing by the window, looking out, as Tessa walked up, wrapped her arms around him, and lay her head on his back. He rubbed his hands over her arms before turning around to wrap her in his arms and place a kiss on the top of her head. Tessa lifted her head and smiled up at him. She reached around his neck and pulled him down to place a kiss on his lips. Logan bent down to lift her up and take control of the kiss. He ran his tongue over her lips. Tessa moaned and opened her mouth as the kiss deepened, and their tongues danced together in a graceful and slow dance. Suddenly, the phone rang. Logan pulled back and placed his forehead on her's before reaching to pick up the phone and flip it open.

"Code 525 here," Logan said, and he waited to hear which code was given in answer.

"Echo 1 reached and placed. All is safe, and your package is now placed on ice. Your attention is needed to release the information, and I have been told to say that Echo 1 is now code 001, sir," the caller said before hanging up. Logan slowly closed the phone and looked up to see that the guys were now in the office and waiting to hear what had happened.

"Code 001, so I guess we are in the clear, and all is good. They need us in Washington, DC, ASAP for a debriefing. Both the director and Joaquin have been arrested and are in cells now with many of the others," Logan said to everyone in the room before looking down at Tessa and picking her up to finish the kiss they had started.

Days later, after many days of debriefing from all departments behind closed doors, Logan was waiting with Nick outside the US marshal office for Tessa. She was still in a meeting with the new director and the new heads of the CIA, FBI, and justice department.

"Why are they taking so long with her? She has been in there for days. What more can she tell them?" Nick said. Logan just stood leaning next to the column. Logan looked up to see Tessa walking out of the building, and his heart nearly stopped as she walked slowly down to meet him. She was wearing a black pencil skirt with a white silk blouse and four-inch heels that did things to her legs that made him moan. Her hair was styled in an up do, making her look stunning. He was not sure which look he liked the most. It was the jeans-wearing woman he had fallen in love with, but this side of her was damn fucking sexy too.

"Hey, handsome, been waiting long?" she said before placing a kiss on his lips. She stepped back and looked at him for a moment to see how he was feeling.

"About fucking time, they let you go. How many ways can you tell them the same fucking story and not get it right?" Nick said, smiling at them. Logan placed an arm around her and pulled her closer. A man came running down the stairs toward them.

"Marshal Miller, I have a request from the president. He would like to invite you and Mr. McMullen to lunch tomorrow. Here is the invitation for you. Please let me know so I can make the arrangements for you," the president's aide said to her. Tessa looked at Logan to ask him what he wanted to do about it. All he did was smile and nod.

"Yes, we would love to have lunch with him. Thank you," she said to the aide before they turned to walk down the steps toward the car that was waiting for them. Just before they reached the car, Logan stopped and pulled Tessa to him. He got down on one knee, took her hand, and pulled out a box. He opened it to reveal a stunning ring with a diamond in the center and blue sapphires on both sides.

"Tessa, you have had my heart from the moment I first met you. I feel complete now with you and could not see a moment in my life without you, so would you do me the honor of making me your husband?" Logan said. While waiting for her answer, he watched as tears filled her eyes. She pressed her lips together and then nodded and said yes. Logan stood, wrapped her in his arms, and kissed her. All around them, they heard people yelling and whistling. Some were clapping their hands as Logan pulled back and placed the ring on her finger.

CHAPTER 20

ON A BEACH SOMEPLACE IN THE Caribbean, the breeze was warm, a full moon was shining down, and the ocean waves gently kissed the beach on which a house sat. In the beach house, Tessa lay with her head on Logan's shoulder with only a sheet covering them. Logan was softly running his hand over her bare back. He kissed her forehead.

"So how is the honeymoon going, Mrs. McMullen?"

Tessa lifted her head and looked into his eyes with a playful smile on her face. "Well, so far, very good. I mean, the place is picturesque, the weather is wonderful, and the company is charming. The only problem is that it will not last forever, Mr. McMullen."

"What do you mean it will not last forever?" he said.

Tessa just laughed and hugged him tighter. "Have I told you how much I love you lately?" she said, rubbing circles over his chest.

Logan continued to rub her back lightly. "Well, not for at least five minutes."

Tessa leaned up on her elbow and looked at him. "I want to thank you."

A confused look moved over his face. "Okay, but what is it you are thanking me for, babe?" he said. Tessa looked at him and took a deep breath.

"You made me whole. I was a broken person. I did not think I would find love, and now you have mended my shattered heart. You never gave up on me and continued to be there even when I did everything to push you away. I am whole only because you loved me and saw me under all that pain and hate. Thank you for that," she said as a tear fell down her face. Logan reached up, brushed it away, leaned over, and kissed her deeply.

"I think I was bewitched from the moment I saw you and touched you. I could never think of not having you. It was fate that we would be together. I could not see my life without you. You see, I love you too much to be without you," he told her, and then he kissed her again.

As Tessa lay back and curled into Logan, she asked, "Do you think Nick is in love with Beth? I mean, at the wedding, they could not keep their eyes off of each other, and they only danced with each other. It was funny to explain to her why she was getting an invitation to our wedding when she thought we were already on our honeymoon. The look on her face was priceless. You do know that Nick is crazy about her, and that is the reason he was mad at you about her leaving, right?" she said as she pulled up to look at him.

"Yes, I was able to figure that out, but I am still not too sure about her. There is something going on with her. I just have a feeling about it. Do you think that your parents will be able to work things out? It seemed like they were at the wedding, and your dad is trying to work his problems out too," Logan said.

"I hope so. I think I have made my peace with him. We had a very long talk, and we both have a lot to forgive each other for, but I think it will be fine. Just think of it as left-handed justice—you do not know where it is coming from until you see it," she told him, smiling up at him.

CPSIA information can be obtained
at www.ICGtesting.com
Printed in the USA
BVHW082229100921
616546BV00008B/466